The Edge

Scott Thomas

Copyrights

ISBN: 978-1-950576-91-3

Cover design by Roger Wilson

Book design and production by David Lewis Kyle

Editing by Jeremiah Davis

Author photograph by Mahogany Smith

Table of Contents

Preface

Faith is an intangible thing. You can call it a feeling, a system, or just belief. Faith means a lot of things for everyone. However, the most common denominator is having something or someone to believe in. There are several religions that preach different things and are more or less the same morally and ethically. The difference lies in the core beliefs of that faith. Now, I won't speak about how other people are impacted by their respective faiths and belief systems, because I can only speak about mine. I am sure it's a positive impact for any believer in some kind of higher power. When it comes to believing in a higher power, you need to know that the one you believe in is the one true Almighty creator and sustainer of the universe and all creation-mankind, and animals. Different religions may lay claim that they are right, and we all have a right to believe in whatever we want, but I here want to make a case for Christianity. I want to do that because it is one faith that has impacted my life beyond measure. Sometimes, a moment in life affects you so much that you start thinking about your life. You start to realize how life has become so material, and we're just working for a living to feed our material desires. Once you realize how your life is so empty because you're living like a machine. You just eat, sleep, work, and it's the same routine every day. It's the same wash cycle.

We're so conditioned, and we don't know how important it is to have spiritual fulfillment. We live and work to feed our bodies, but what about the soul. One can't exist without the other, and both are equal parts of our existence. So, the question I pose is: how can you feed your soul? What can make the heart feel content? We are never going to be completely happy and content with our lives unless we don't have soul fulfillment. I felt the same when I lost my job and had to face the music of being unemployed and having to tell my wife and family. The pain was real, but there was a bigger pain I was not aware of. My soul was crying because my priorities were the same as before I got laid off. They were simply to get a job and earn a living and work like a machine. I didn't realize that it was a turning point in my life. It was what one would consider is a transition too. No matter what you may call it, it's a time of realization. It's time to look back at your life and do a self–assessment. It's time to take a hard look at yourself and see where you have patches in spirituality. The truth is that I had not just lost my job. I had lost the edge. I had lost that spiritual edge that my soul had been crying for so long. It was a moment in time that led me to believe that there is a greater purpose to life than just living like a machine.

I realized that I had forgotten the existence of a higher power in my life. It was time that I spoke to my soul so I could figure out what it needed. My soul called to me and pointed me to my true calling. I picked up the Holy Bible and started to read. I kept on reading, and I found the answers I was seeking. I found that there was a higher power that was known to all believers as our

Lord and Savior Jesus Christ. In order to bring back that edge, I needed to transform myself into a believer. I had to submit myself solely to the will of our Heavenly Father. The Christian God is The Father, the Son, and the Holy Spirit, all in one. It's one being with three persons. They represent the Holy Trinity. Our Lord and Savior Jesus Christ died on the cross for our sins. His death and resurrection meant our sins have been completely washed away and belief in Him means that we are all gifted with eternal salvation. It's a beautiful feeling, and once you hold on to the rope of our Lord and Savior Jesus Christ, you see life in such a different light. All our worldly problems seem so small, and you're enriched with so much spiritual energy to take on the world. You can tackle life's greatest problems by just believing in God and let Him pave the way forward for you. That's how you regain that spiritual edge once you strengthen the connection with Him and maintain it very tightly. Nothing can stand in your way. That, my friends, is the power of faith. Faith is a very beautiful thing to have. It's such a powerful feeling. It can truly move mountains.

This book you are about to read talks about regaining that spiritual edge that has been lost somewhere. It is lost because we have become so lost in the material world we live in. We have no time for God even though we do know of and believe in His existence. That's why I don't look back at my job loss with negativity but with pride. That was the day I started walking the path of God. That's when I realized my life had a greater purpose. Now, whatever life I have left is dedicated to walking that path and becoming spiritually enlightened. That's the way forward to be a better believer, a Christian, and a human being. The book will cover the various phases that are part of this voyage of discovery or rediscovery. It's an evolutionary process and is filled with transitions and turning points. You should never be afraid to call yourself a born-again Christian. This is because everyone in this situation is experiencing a spiritual rebirth, so such labels don't need to impact us in the wrong way. It's about reaching out to God and filling the spiritual holes in your life. The scripture that would be referenced throughout the book would be II Kings 6: 1-

7. I will also be illustrating my points with examples from real life. A lot of us face similar situations in life. Some are tough, and some are easy, and some would be so crazy that they could potentially take us on a dark path. This is why this book is so important. By giving you examples from real life and Scripture, you can be on the right path of growth, maturity, and spiritual enlightenment. So, this way, you get the best of both worlds.

As you know that we are living in the times of the COVID-19 pandemic- the coronavirus disease- and this is a time where everyone all over the world has perhaps lost hope of traditional medicine and science because there seems no solution to the pandemic. We are living in what is being called the new normal. The coronavirus disease is going to stay, and we have to live with it until a vaccine isn't found. Now, if this isn't a transition and a turning point in our lives, then I wouldn't know what else to call it. It's the biggest test of strength and spirituality of human beings. This is one test that not all of us have passed. Some of our friends, loved ones, kith, and kin, have all passed away due to the disease. Now, we can't let their passings go in vain. We need to realize that they didn't pass away because they were spiritually weak. It could be that God wanted them near to Him and leave most of us behind to pave the way for others. We can say that God is angry with us because we have lost faith. We have gone down the dark path, and this pandemic is a way to get us back to the path of our Lord and Savior Jesus Christ. The truth is different, at least in my opinion. I firmly believe that God is infinitely merciful and loves us more than our parents and our spouses. He would never be upset with us. He is just calling us to his path in these uncertain times so we can regain our spiritual edge. A lot of us have become lost souls in these uncertain times. No one knows when this will end as it could be with us for the next few years. This may be the best time for all us lost souls to return to God. If we look at this turning point as a means of a spiritual revolution, then together, we can beat the coronavirus disease. This is because faith is a great healer. Furthermore, there is nothing greater than faith in God Almighty. These uncertain times are a reminder that life is too short, and we need to make the most of this time we have on our beloved planet. We should return to God and reignite our spirituality so we can become better Christians and better human beings. Once we have reached the highest stage of enlightenment, we can better tackle this pandemic. We should not let it dictate our lives but use this opportunity to return to walking the path of our Lord and Savior Jesus Christ.

By referencing the Scriptures, we can find answers to questions that are previously unknown to us. Our Holy Bible is a beacon of knowledge, the stories and lessons are so practical, and if we think deep enough, we realize that these are our stories. These are the stories that can teach us how to tackle the mysteries of the universe. More specifically, it will explain why things happen to us. You must know that God will only make us endure what we can bear. Sometimes, it can be a lot, but He knows that we can go the distance if we seek His help and knowledge. The way to gain connected to God is to study the Scriptures and harness the knowledge within them. There is so much we don't even know, and there is so much we need to learn and teach others. I was brought to this realization, and that's what led me to study the Scriptures and eventually write this book. It was the ultimate voyage of discovery for me, and I learned a lot through this time. I learned so much about the Holy Trinity, especially our Lord and Savior Jesus Christ. Through the stories of the Old Testament prophets, I learned how they tackled situations that presented to them as transitions and turning points. I would read about them and analyze them. I would also study them deeply and try to apply the knowledge I gained in my life so I can tell you all while writing this book. The knowledge I gained is something that is so practical, and I wanted to explain it to you in simple language so that everyone who is reading can understand clearly. I would apply it to modern-day logic and thinking, so there could be practical applications for all of us today. I felt that by understanding the messages contained in the Scriptures, we can fill the spiritual holes in our lives and regain the edge.

My hope is when you read that book, you begin the same journey that I embarked on. If you are already on that journey and have experienced a spiritual rebirth, then more power to you. My prayers are with all of you, and have full faith in God that He has a plan for all of us. One thing I must leave you before you start the opening chapter of this book is that it is not us that makes the changes we require in life. It is God. We must embrace the change because, at the end of the day, we're not just making an impact in our lives, but for our near, dear, and loved ones too. Always remember, there can be miracles when you believe, as sung by Mariah Carey and Whitney Houston in the soundtrack of the hit Disney animated movie "The Prince of Egypt." Hallelujah!

Overview: Recovering Spiritual Sharpness

"Give me six hours to chop down a tree, and I will spend the first four sharpening the ax." — Abraham Lincoln

"If the iron be blunt and you do not whet the edge, then you have to put forth more strength, but wisdom is more profitable to direct." — Ecclesiastes 10:10 (KJV).

There is a cry reverberating from the heart of God to the soul of the church, bellowing his longing for his people to rediscover their spiritual edge. In a period where the church is experiencing unusual manifestations of both his power and grace, there is a growing sense that many within the corridors of the sacred assembly have lost their personal "cutting-edge" and are hopelessly swinging between the pendulum of theological desperation and spiritual dullness.

It is this spiritual dullness that is examined. Why are so many of our Christian leaders and members experiencing longs periods of dryness? Countless believers are keeping their normal routines of attending church regularly, participating in small-group discipleship gatherings, and serving in various ministries as their time permits. However, gnawing at the corner of their souls is a frightening realization that something has created a sense of bluntness within the expression of their Christian experience.

In an age where superficial Christianity is worn as an entitled mantle rather than a shameful robe, we within Christendom should not be alarmed that many disciples that are being birthed in today's Church lack the spiritual fortitude to maintain their sharpness when the trials of life begin to stifle their effectiveness. Subsequently, more people are finding themselves spending time grasping the horns of the altar, or buried in the confines of counseling sessions with little or no change.

Leaders in all sects of the faith are searching for answers to aid them in the fight to strengthen their people in maintaining their sharp spiritual posture. While some of these leaders are suggesting that their followers perform a spiritual inventory to try to uncover the source of their dullness, often, the leader's suggested attempt ends in frustration because the follower has neglected to focus on the right areas to discover the pathology of their dullness. Thus, the following book seeks to depict how many have fallen prey to spiritual dullness, while still seeking a pastor, teach, lead, and simply serve during their Christian journey. Moreover, the contents of the treatise provide the practical steps to rediscover your personal "edge," during wilderness type seasons that are calculated to push you towards the God-edge – microcosms of frustrating and undefined experiences designated by the Master to help you and me measure our sharpness at any given state. The pain and hurt that is attributed to losing your personal edge is daunting, even for the mature and strong within the faith. For a few, the possibility of facing such a dilemma strikes a guttural piercing chord at the essence of their heart.

Furthermore, men especially have difficulty in voicing their frustration when discussing issues that are rooted within their manhood, and often are fearful in communicating with other brothers that their struggle has contributed to the loss of their personal edge. Buried deep underneath the reservoir of reluctance, many men yearn with tears to understand what has restricted them to tap their transparent vein and communicate their need for meaningful relationships that can aid them in re-discovery of their sharpness. Moreover, women, who traditionally find it easier to communicate a narrative that includes the tapestry of their emotional intel woven with spiritual décor, are discovering the difficulty to voice their personal battles with losing their edge with their sisterly counter-parts.

Personally, having served in various leadership roles within both the church and corporate settings, maintaining my spiritual edge has always been a wrestling encounter with God. Like Jacob of old, I have often crossed over the metaphoric Jabbok River within my life only to find a Christ waiting on the other side, armed and dangerous, holding my name change on the proverbial tip of his tongue, but he was hesitant to vocalize it because of my resistance to succumb to his strength in his presence. My lust, my lies, and my limitations kept me imprisoned and impotent to wield the sharp ax-head of his glory. Deceptively inviting was the temptation to limp through life under a false premise that forgiveness was all that was needed, without a context of restitution attached to my "confessed" change. I had lost the "sharp-edge" - the battle-ax of his power, necessary to cut through the forest of disillusionment within my life. I needed to rediscover the edge!

This book uses as a backdrop, the story found in II Kings 6:1-7, to highlight the process of the sudden loss and recovery of the ax-head by one under the discipleship of Elisha within the school of the prophets.

Principles extrapolated from the narrative undergird the importance of how both expected and unexpected transitions play in both lost and recovery efforts in discipleship. Reflective questions summarize the end of each chapter to aid the reader in evaluating how the principles within the chapter are applicable to their personal journey. Finally, a workbook is provided to help individuals within small group bible studies to examine the passages and discuss the implications of loss recovery. Don't take this book as just a self-help book but take it as a manual. This manual is here to help you reach deep down inside and find that inner voice that has been quiet for so very long. You want it to speak to you and tell you that it needs to be heard and understood. Once that communication has been initiated, then the journey to rediscover your edge will start. That voice is speaking the truth to you. This is the truth you have ignored for most of your life because you are experiencing spiritual dullness. This spiritual dullness is holding you back from reaching your maximum potential as a Christian and as a human being.

You need to hear that inner voice and lift yourself up spiritually as I have done to rediscover my lost edge. You can find it too and reconnect with our Lord and Savior, Jesus Christ and then learn to hold on to His rope and walk His path. These are very essential things for every Christian who wants to stay connected with the Carpenter of the Universe Jesus Christ. This book is not about my journey, but it's about our journey as Christians, and it is my hope that I can educate you with this on how to rekindle that spirituality that has been hidden somewhere in the depths of our heart as we steer our lives in this material world. Trust me when I tell you this, there will be hard times as you already may have known. Those times are our tests and trials, and we should never be afraid to face them. One thing you all must remember and realize. That one thing is that what doesn't kill you only makes you stronger. That exactly is the point of these tests and trials we face in our lives. These are designed to make us stronger individuals and better Christians. We aren't the only ones who have faced tests and trials. We will continue to face them all our lives, and that has happened to everyone who has come before us and will come after us as well. Our prophets have been tested, and so was our Lord and Savior, Jesus Christ. We need to learn from their stories to become better Christians as well as better human beings. I would go further and say that we should become so spiritually strong that we can face our lives' challenges head-on and tackle them with all our strengths in full force. You see, faith is very powerful, and it certainly can move mountains- metaphorically speaking. If your faith is strong and untouchable, then nothing is impossible in life. You can't be shaken or broken. That's the power of faith, and it's quite incredible; I must tell you. You will learn through reading the next several chapters as to how you can rebuild and re-strengthen that bond with our Lord and Savior Jesus Christ and sustain that connection with him your entire life. You will learn how to make the best decisions in tough times in light of those prophets that came before us and what we can learn from the decisions they have made. We will be going through each chapter with references to passages from our Holy Bible, and that includes both the Old and New Testaments.

God's love is so immense and zealous that he is committed to a reckless pursuit of you and me to gain back that sharp ax in the Spirit. No matter the story, you have been designed, developed, and destined to swing within intention the ax of Christ's power to overcome all opposition and obstacles that are calculated to impinge you from accomplishing his intent within your life. My hope is that you read this book with a heart settled to understand with the revelation that you were meant to live on the Edge!

1

Small, Slim, & Slender Spaces

"Gritty people train at the edge of their comfort zone. They zero in on one narrow aspect of their performance and set a stretch goal to improve it." — Angela Duckworth

The company of the prophets said to Elisha, "Look, the place where we meet with you is too small for us." — 2 Kings 6:1 (NIV).

Opening my car door was one of the most difficult tasks on this day because I knew the long drive home would require me to reflect on how to communicate to my wife how we would survive this recent news that I had once again lost my job as a federal contractor. I was a victim of the ebbs and flows connected to a career that relies upon the winds of insincere relationships blowing in the empty corridors of old government buildings primarily located within Washington, D.C. While the anticipated conversation with my wife was disheartening, the greater concern was the inevitable "feeling" of constriction that would reverberate within my soul like the sound of a stringed instrument being plucked by an amateur musician. This narrow restrained "sense" encapsulated my thoughts, plundering me into a reality that the four walls of my world seemed to be slowly closing in on my life. At that point, there was no way out of my predicament. I had to face the music and give in to fate. I also had to think of restarting my life now that my job was gone. It was back to square one, and I had to start from scratch. Anyone in my position would feel the same way. They would feel that the world is crashing down on them and that their life is over. There is no picking yourself up from this. There is no motivation at all to get up and change things. This is a very crucial time in any person's life. It's a time when your faith in our Lord and Savior Jesus Christ is also tested. These tests come now and again in our lives. Our lives are very challenging, and each person deals with those challenges in different ways. We can either give up or take charge of our life. Taking charge may not be the easiest decision to take at the time, but if you look inside yourself and reach down deep inside and hear that inner voice. It will speak to you and tell me that all is not lost yet. You can still live your life, but this time you will have to uncover spiritual dullness in your life and sharpen those edges. This way, you can reconnect with our Lord and Savior Jesus Christ and re-strengthen that bond. Once that bond is formed, there is no turning back. You can live your life, and you will see that it's self-fulfilling. You will see it first-hand just as I did. I would like you to understand where I am coming from and relate your experiences to mine so that you can learn from it. As a Christian, I feel that if I have knowledge and experience that help and guide other Christians in sharpening areas of their lives where there is spiritual dullness, then I feel I have done my duty.

However, while a loss of a job was not the end of the world for me, it meant that things may begin to get tight and narrow as my finances were being squeezed to maintain our family lifestyle. I knew cutbacks and modified lifestyle decisions were mandatory. These changes are part and parcel of such life changes. These are also necessary at such times, even though they would be only temporary until I am back on my feet again financially. Nevertheless, a very important spiritual principle was being downloaded to me from the Spirit of God concerning "narrow places." How does God use narrow spaces and places to perfect his people in the kingdom? This was a discovery I made, and this pretty much changed my life from that point on. It's always important to look back on how the prophets tackled problems with the grace of Christ. They knew God's grace was always with them, and they held no fear at all whatsoever. That's the same principle and attitude we need to adopt in our lives too to tackle problems. These examples in the Scriptures are for our own benefit and no one else. By using these as reference points, we can better understand the role in our life of our Lord and Savior Jesus Christ. We can also seek inspiration from these stories and learn to better improve ourselves as well. These stories are designed to teach us lessons and apply them to our daily lives so we can be better Christians and human beings. I feel that life is a constant journey of self- improvement. At every step of this journey, you have to check yourself and see if you're making the right decisions, and you have to keep looking towards our Lord and Savior Jesus Christ for answers. He knows more than us, and he will guide us at all times, and it doesn't matter if we are alone or with people. He doesn't discriminate. At the end of the day, we are all God's children. See, there is only one constant in life, and that is change. We are always changing, even though we may not be aware of those changes. We are changing inside and outside as we grow and live our lives. Change is inevitable, and we need to embrace change because until we don't, we can't improve ourselves at all. Life is a journey where we will change so much, and we will reach a point where we may not remember or recognize how we used to be. The past is something that can't be undone or changed. However, the present and future are in our hands. We can control that, and we can direct ourselves to walk the path of our Lord and Savior Jesus Christ. I must tell you that it's never too late. We just need to reconnect with Him and re-strengthen that bond. Once that bond is re-strengthened and cemented, then you will be guided at every turn of your life, and you will be able to embrace that change much easier. You will also be able to make the best decisions for yourself, your loved ones, your family, friends, and all those impacted by your decisions. The best part is that they will learn from you, and when they will see your point and exercise on your teachings, they will see the true power in finding that lost edge. Once they have regained their connection with our Lord and Savior Jesus Christ, they will be able to pass on their knowledge to others who require it. Time and again, we should be keeping our faith and spirituality in check because it's easy to get distracted by the superficial attractions of the modern material world we live in. We can lose focus, and that's the time we need to regain that connection and re-strengthen that bond with our Lord and Savior Jesus Christ. That will make sure we are constantly walking His path and improving our lives.

Elisha, the Prophet of God, was an overseer of a school of budding prophets, tasked with the leadership responsibility of disciplining and training the next generation of ministers within Israel. In second Kings, the sixth chapter, the school of the prophets was dwelling most likely in either Gilgal or Jericho. This training environment was starting to receive notoriety and exposure, attracting other prophetic disciples to the location. Thus, with the addition of new ministers joining the ranks of the brotherhood, the "space" where they met became increasingly narrow and small. The tight quarters that the trainees were experiencing necessitated a unified response, which suggested that Elisha consider allowing them as an organization to seek a new location for the company prophets to continue their training.

"What happens spiritually when the places and spaces within your life are starting to become narrow and slim?" The feeling of constriction within your personal world, while uncomfortable, often plays a major role in preparing you and me for changes and transitions that are on the horizon. The sense that your life is slowly closing in on all sides, while you must still function normally with your day-to-day routine can be disheartening and confusing. Many Christians become disillusioned under the intense pressure that is created from the smothering effects felt when life begins to narrow and tighten. Whether the "narrowing effect" is a result of a job loss, a discovered health issue, or a recent divorce, it is imperative to filter your decisions and responses through the wisdom of Christ. By following God's wisdom during seasons of constriction can expedite the time-frame in which you and I are required to experience this narrowness within our lives.

However, narrow seasons are utilized by Christ to position us for expansion. Thus, the first principle of this book is revealed:

"God leverages small and slender spaces within our life to examine our spiritual sharpness!"

The small and slender spaces in our life are calculated to make us cry out to the Carpenter of the Universe to help us discover a new location to expand and grow. Small mental and spiritual spaces are designed to frustrate the believer by irritating them to the degree that it causes a deliberate request to ascend from the well of the soul in the form of supplication prayer. It causes us to reach out to the being that created us and brought us into this world and gave us a life to live with family, friends, material possessions, and more. It makes us more human than human beings we have become. We have become too wrapped up by the outside world, and we seem to forget God, who has constantly been watching over us since we were born and up till now. We need to rediscover our bond with Christ and re-establish our association with Him. I'm sure when you're reading this, you have tons of questions in your mind. Mostly these questions are related to faith and Christ and His place in our lives.

Sometimes we may feel that God has left us, and we feel distant. When there's too much going wrong, where is God to fix our problems? Why doesn't he hear our prayers? Is He really out there? These questions become burning questions in our minds, and we start questioning our faith. It's those times our faith is tested, and we have to be strong. That's what separates true believers from believers. The true believers' faiths will be tested, but they will not waiver from the right path. They know that eventually, God will come to their aid. It's about not taking God for granted. Everything is fine and dandy when we're living it up, and life is great. But whenever we are knee-deep in problems, we will call on Him for help and wait for him to answer our prayers. At that time, we need to be steadfast in our beliefs and work hard to make things right. In the end, with His grace, we will pull through. We have to hold on to His rope no matter what. Pastor Andy Stanley, via Christian Post, was quoted as saying, "If you're on edge... if you have your doubts ... my challenge to you is to draw back into the simple story and the teaching of Jesus." Stanley was even quoted as saying, "God says I want everyone to experience my forgiveness. What God wants ... is to restore the relationship." Several prophets and messengers saw hard times during their preaching days, but that never forced them to waver from their path. The saying here makes sense: what doesn't kill you only makes you stronger. Hence, they held steadfast to their faith against all the odds and were ultimately rewarded. We need to follow in their footsteps and meet the challenges life throws at us in the same way. Then we will realize that no problem is too big or too small.

In Genesis 21:19, "Then Christ opened her eyes, and she saw a well of water. So she went and filled the skin with water and gave the boy a drink" we see how Christ rewarded Hagar's patience, and she was able to hydrate her young child. Similarly, if we stay patient throughout our tough times, then Christ will open our eyes too, and so shall we see too just like the righteous ones before us did. It's important that we trust in God that He is with us and will make it right as long as we keep our faith alive. It's a battle of wills, and that's how our faith is tested. It eventually gets us closer to God. As long as our faith is strong as it was with Hagar, we will find the well of water we are seeking. We don't need to give up hope at all. We need to be firm and steadfast in our faith and walk the path of our Lord and Savior, Jesus Christ. We will ultimately find the solutions to our problems and be confident and strong at all times. No problem, big or small, will be a hurdle for us.

The ultimate goal is to be close to him, and since we are destined for everlasting life, we should feel more comfortable knowing our fate is in the right hands. We have nothing to fear because we are walking the path of God, and no matter what happens on the way, we'll have His blessings on every turn. No matter the problems we face, we will always have His love to pull us through. We just have to hold on to His rope as tight as possible and never let go. Once we've held tight, we'll have nothing to worry about us because we have held the rope of the being that created us and which has given us the privilege to live the lives we are living. This doesn't mean we won't be tested. We'll be tested time and again, but its how we pull ourselves out of those tests or conquer them is where our faith is actually tested. We can always take God for granted, and that's when we realized how there's no color in life anymore. With Christ, there's light because His light shines on us always as long as we hold steadfast to His rope.

I lost my job, and this was my test of faith. However, I held on to the rope of Christ, knowing that some life changes will be necessary. I even held the belief that something better will come my way. I was dreading telling my wife, but this is life. It's not perfect. It keeps throwing us curveballs. This is just one of those curveballs. Once this tough phase passes, life will be back to normal or even better. Some people may turn to drugs and alcohol and become depressed after losing their livelihood. What good would that get anyone? It only makes things worse. Belief in Christ is the way. We stay patient, modify our life as needed, pray, and eventually, things will come full circle. If we keep the faith, things will get better. So many people lose their job daily, and while it may seem hard and the road ahead looks tough. Worrying about it won't make things better or undo anything. It gives us newfound energy that there is someone watching over us, and we have to stay strong through such times, and that's only when patience gets rewarded. We need to rise above all this and rediscover our purpose in life. That purpose is to walk in Christ's path. It's the way to everlasting life, and that's bigger than any job or otherworldly accomplishments.

You may find your fellow brothers and sisters caught in the same situation. Then you can remind them of Galatians 6:1, which says, "Brethren, even if anyone is caught in any trespass, you who are spiritual, restore such a one in a spirit of gentleness; each one looking to yourself so that you too will not be tempted." This is your chance to show them that if their faith is restored, better things will happen to them, and their patience will be rewarded in due course. This is not the time to rebuke them for their lack of faith but shower them with love and kindness, just like Christ showers us with the same. With the right amount of care, these brothers and sisters will find healing power in faith. Patience is key as the way our life is structured, there's always some problem or the other to deal with. We need to be there for each other in these times. This is how we can share Christ's love with our brethren. We're all part of His kingdom and one family. We need to talk to these brothers and sisters, counsel them, and keep reminding them that God is with them. This time will pass. If we fill them with positive thinking, then we are benefiting them as well as us. Negative emotions only lead to self-destruction, and that takes us away from Christ. Every person takes their time to heal, and it is in those days, love, care, and attention goes a long way. Reading passages from the Bible, whether Old or New Testament, helps them. Forming support groups is even better as they can talk to others suffering from similar issues and how their faith has helped them to stay strong through tough times. Believing is only half the battle, but staying strong and the patient is the other. Once we've mastered both, then we have found spiritual peace. At the same time, when the craziness is over, we should still hold steadfast to our faith. Our lives are a never-ending struggle, so the stronger our grip is on our faith, the easier our lives are. Attending church regularly, participating in Bible study, support groups, youth groups, and other ways of fellowship help us stay true to our faith because we are among those that are like us, and our aim is to bring the lost back to God. God loves us all of us, and every lost soul can be turned back towards him. Being lost gives us a chance at redemption and rediscovering faith. It is a journey in itself. Once our eyes are reopened, they will never close because God's love and grace will be shining on us all. When that light shines on us, we will realize how small our problems are because we would have learned to rise above them and become better human beings and Christians as a result.

I must tell you something very important. It's never too late to turn to God. It could take us the last year of our lives to turn to our Lord and Savior Jesus Christ. He is waiting for us to turn to him. See, I lost a job to realize I needed to turn to Jesus Christ. I realized that I am powerless without Him. There is nothing we can do in life if it is not His will. See, faith can move mountains, but to first build faith, you need to believe. You need to make that connection with our Heavenly Father, and only then will things be going into motion. You need to kickstart the process by first having faith in our Lord and Savior, Jesus Christ, and then pray to Him constantly. That way, you will be able to fill holes in your spirituality. Prayer is also very powerful. It is the most powerful weapon that you have. You have to realize that we are all God's children. He will never let us down, and He knows us more and better than we know ourselves. You will see a natural fulfillment in your lives because you have taken the first step to eternal salvation. First comes belief and then comes prayer, and then comes action. It's a three-step process, and it's the most incredible journey you can take in life. In the following chapters, you will learn what steps to take in regard to these three mains steps so you can find your spiritual edge again. All of us feel lost and confused at several times in our lives. We feel all alone as there is no one there to help us out in our problems. You don't even need to turn to anyone but our Lord and Savior Jesus Christ. He is the be all and end all of everything. He is the Alpha and the Omega. You need to feel it inside you. You need to feel it in every inch of your bones. Every ounce and energy you have will have the divine power within you, and that all comes from faith. It's an unlimited and infinite source of energy that you have at your disposal. It's the most amazing feeling you can ever have in your life. I know it may be hard to believe, but to be honest, it's not. Once you take that first step, everything else becomes clear. You can and will recover your spiritual edge. The most powerful being in the universe is at your side, so why do you have to worry about anything at all! The answer lies within the faith, and that's all you need to do to recover your edge. Things will fall into place, and you will surprise yourself and the people around you. Everyone around will see the divine light reflecting from your persona, and that is an incredibly powerful feeling. It comes to you at no cost because faith is priceless. It is true that in life, there is no such thing as a free lunch. However, belief in our Lord and Savior is the one free lunch you can have multiple times in your life. It keeps on giving and giving. You should make this book your guide because all I am telling you is what I have experienced. I have fully experienced the divine power of our Lord and Savior Jesus Christ inside me and have thus recovered my spiritual edge. Not only that, my spirituality has increased ten-fold. You will see the same change in yourself. I took that first step and started believing. It didn't take much time for things to turn in my favor because I saw God's work in front of my very own eyes. I took the right steps based on the divine guidance I received, and that is when I saw that I had become simply one with God. That is the end goal I want you all to have. If you have gotten this far already, then more power to you. But, do read on as you can discover different ways of increasing your spirituality even further, 80s pop diva Cyndi Lauper once sang. “If you’re lost, you can look, and you will find me... time after time.” That is exactly what our Lord and Savior Jesus Christ want us to do. We all are lost souls, at least most of us. We will find Him if we look, and to look, we need to have faith and make that connection strong. That’s how we can build our relationship with our Heavenly Father.

The purpose of this book is to help us find our spiritual sharpness and rediscover it if it's lost. God tests us through the small, slender, and narrow spaces. I've been tested, and so shall you be as you move along in life. So many of us have been tested before, and we need to learn how to adapt and persevere. Most of all, we have to keep our faith strong in God that throughout the testing times, He only wants the best for us. If we stay patient and persevere, we will see God's plan, and then we will think differently about those tough times. It showed how we returned to Him during these times of duress and looked to Him. He showed us the way, and we found our calling. Throughout the following chapters, you will learn how to rediscover that spiritual edge back. We will talk about different ways that can happen and how you have been tested and will be tested. Thank you for joining me on this journey to rediscover your edge!

2

Transitions, Turning Points, & Transformations

"It's no use going back to yesterday because I was a different person then." — Lewis Carroll, Alice in Wonderland

"Please let us go to the Jordan, and let every man take a beam from there, and let us make there a place where we may dwell." — II Kings 6:2

The focused scripture indicates that the school of prophets needed to transition from the narrow place where their training was currently located to a place that could support their growing attendance. Subsequently, many of our life's choices hinge on small turning points within our lives. These decisions, while small in nature, are adjustments that help navigate our paths towards our overall destiny. Each decision that we make during times of change enables us to gain greater insight into Christ's plan for our lives. Whether we experience transition through a divorce, financial upheaval, or a new health episode, our faith in Jesus Christ will ultimately help us through the transition. "Spiritual dullness is sleepy thinking. It's a listless state of thought that fails to get anything significant accomplished." It's when one feels less inspired spiritually, and there is a lack of progress on that side. We need to fill the void that comes with the spiritual dullness that comes in our life. We need to get close to Christ to reinstate the spiritual fulfillment in our life.

In the first chapter, we saw how Elisha's company of prophets asked him to find a larger place for their worship because the current place was too small. This was a turning point as they had to make a transition to a larger space. It was during this time, patience and faith in Christ were needed, and that would automatically restore and re-enhance the relationship with Him. Transformations can normally be dealt with positively and negatively, depending on what they were. For example, I could have gone into depression after losing my job turning to drugs and alcohol, and, in turn, lose respect in front of my wife. It would also show I am a weak man who can't endure challenges because life is full of them. Losing a job is just one of those challenges. There are even worse, such as losing a loved one at an early age or even one at an elderly age, especially if you're closer to them. Most of the time, the grief in losing loved ones can be so much that people get severely affected. That's the time one needs to hold on to the rope of Christ the most. If Christ takes a loved one from us early, it's because he wants that person with Him. So we should trust in Him that he always has the best intentions for us. Sometimes we have seen that our parents give us tough love and force us to do things we don't like. We can disagree with them and be rebellious, but that doesn't help us in any way. Parents generally love their children more than anything else in the world, and they would never want to harm them. Just like we need to have faith and trust in them, we need to have the same trust and faith in our Lord too. He created the heavens and the earth, and he created us, so every challenge He throws us is to make us more close to Him. It is, after all, to Him we shall return after we die. Transitions are a normal part of life, and we're always in that state whether we realize it or not.

We need to find that fulfillment in the small, slender, and slim spaces, and that's where we will see our faith rejuvenated. Jesus Christ died for our sins so we can be saved. And that is the same example we need to follow. We need to rise up to that level to get that ultimate fulfillment that our lives may lack sometimes. I had lost my job but knew it wasn't the end; it was time for a new beginning. It was the small space I rediscovered that fulfillment because I raised myself to that level that nothing comes closer than faith. It keeps us strong on our darkest days, and we are thankful when days are the brightest. It's about that eternal love and salvation we are blessed to have as Christians. We find ourselves to be inspired by Christ in times where we see no way out.

There's always a way out. And that way out is given us to by our faith. Our faith will lead us home. We can rejuvenate our faith on a daily basis by resisting sin and embrace all that's good. It's not an easy battle to resist sin, but knowing that we will only be in Christ's good grace is a really good incentive for us. Walking in Christ's path means being good Samaritans all over. It's the reason we are on this Earth, to begin with, to grow the kingdom of Christ by showing the same love to others that Christ bestows us on us. Christ has created us for a reason, and the more we share His love with our fellow brothers and sisters and bring them to Jesus so they can be saved as we have been. We need to give them the gift of everlasting life so they can hold strong to the rope of Christ in times of transitions and transformations. We need to let them know that during times of discomfort, they will find their faith leading them home when they're at their narrowest edge.

These sentiments are echoed in Angela Duckworth's quote, which says, "Gritty people train at the edge of their comfort zone. They zero in on one narrow aspect of their performance and set a stretch goal to improve it." We need to find our comfort zone when we are at the edge, at times when our faith is tested. It's always being tested, and it's at the edge when it's tested the most. We have to keep setting ourselves to that higher standard each and every time. There's always room for improvement, and that's where we keep finding that fulfillment that keeps us striving for betterment in our lives. We have to find new comfort zones. Once we realize we're too comfortable, that's when we need to escape that comfort zone and find a new one. We need to continuously seek Christ in each aspect of our lives. We can't leave Christ confined in just our Church gatherings or the Sunday service. God is everywhere, so we should seek Him everywhere. We need to find God in all the small, slender, and slim spaces. He doesn't need to only dwell in the Church, but our hearts. Once we realize that God is with us at all times, we will know that we just need to simply reach out to Him and be steadfast in faith as and we need His guidance. At the end of the day, like our parents, He knows even better what's best for us and what our true calling is. This is why trust in the Lord is of utmost importance, and that's when things get easier. Christ loves us, and we need to keep that in mind at all times because once we do, we have no fear absolutely at all. We have freed ourselves of all distractions and problems because we trust in Him first and foremost.

We, as humans, find ourselves in liminal spaces. According to Better help, liminal is derived from the Latin word limen, which means threshold. It means being in a state of transition; you're either here or there, but somewhere in the middle. In many ways, we can see our lives as a liminal space as we're transitioning from our worldly life to the afterlife. The idea is that life puts us in liminal spaces as I was thrown into one after I lost my job. I was no longer employed and would be seeking employment. I was in that time where I was simply transitioning from having a job to not having one to looking for one. This was a transformative phase for me in my life. It's through these transitional and transformative phases where we need to reconnect with our faith. We will find our path once that relationship is re-established. The job I lost and what happened then was a turning point in my life. Christ puts us in situations like these, so our faith is constantly being tested. In such situations, we can just lose focus and drift to the wrong path, and that can sometimes lead to self-destructive behavior. No one wants to go down that path, but when we are lost and confused, we will drift away from our Lord and Savior Jesus Christ. Life is not a bed of roses, and while every rose has its thorn, we need to navigate our lives to avoid those thorns. We have to find our path by walking in His light. When we meditate and focus on our faith and the Creator, where we're just neither here nor there but in the liminal space. We put ourselves in a liminal space where we are free from all distractions and worries and have a direct connection to Christ. That's the space we should strive to be in from time to time. We can focus all our energies on Him as if time and space have stopped for us. Once we've put our focus on Him, then everything falls in place. Things automatically start working out because we've put our trust and faith in Him. One thing we need to keep in mind is that God will never test us with something we can't handle. No matter how hard any problem is in life, it's something human beings can handle. Whether it's the stress of exams, school, marriage, loss of loved ones, work, unemployment, or even medical illnesses, it's something that we can manage if we keep ourselves steadfast in the faith. It might seem hard, but to be honest, it's not at all because truly, as it has been said before, faith can move mountains. Just imagine how strong and mighty mountains are, but our faith in our Lord and Savior Jesus Christ is even stronger. He can do anything, and our faith will move mountains if we believe strong enough and constantly look up to Him for guidance. Believe me, when I tell you this, it's all in mind. Once you have faith in our Lord and Savior Jesus Christ, everything falls in place.

There are times when we go through a tough transition, such as losing a loved one or the end of a relationship. I would say that's even worse than losing a job because you can still get employed later even if there is time in between the next job and the one you lost. Loved ones and family members can't be replaced because once they're gone, they're gone. Even relationships may never be mended, or if they do, it's not the same anymore. There may be a lot of work required on both ends to restore the relationship. Both events affect us emotionally and can really be hard to get up and recover from. The emotional healing will take time, and the after-effects can be self-destructive if not managed properly. It could lead to depression, substance abuse, and alcohol abuse. These are perhaps the toughest transitions that would make something like even homelessness feel smaller. You may find a new relationship, and even though it may become special, you may at times miss your past relationships too because they too were special at some time. These emotions can result in negative behavior, and we need to be very careful in not letting our emotions getting the best of ourselves. More than relationships, losing loved ones is extremely hard. These can't be replaced at all, and the hurt is so strong that we would become isolated and depressed and harm ourselves like never before. The same kind of self-destructive behavior mentioned above can be taken to the very extreme, and I would include suicidal thoughts as well. These are times when our confidence, self-esteem, and emotional health is very low. Stress and tension levels are very high, and there is a constant feeling of hopelessness. These feelings are constantly hovering us, and we can't seem to get rid of them in any way. We e can't help but keep thinking about them, and they start controlling our thoughts and emotions. We seem to be so tied up in them that we can't break the chains at all. The more we try, the harder it gets. We just start sinking deep into depression, and it starts taking a heavy toll on us physically and emotionally. At times like these, you are presented with a handful of choices. You can either sink deeper into the sandpit or try to get up and be strong again, both physically and emotionally. The former is easy, but the latter is a lot harder. You may wonder how that is possible. Sinking deep is simply the start within you, the way you are, and not willing to change anything in yourself. We'll discuss later why change is the only constant in life, but here I want to stress that change starts within you first. And you may be wondering how that change can happen or take place. That inner change can come with belief and faith in our Lord and Savior Jesus Christ, who is constantly watching over us. Even as Christians, we do lose our way and can get caught in the same sandtrap as anyone else. For that, we need to constantly stay in touch with our Lord and Savior, Jesus Christ, and look to him for guidance. He is the key to finding peace in our minds and hearts. Once we seek him out, once the connection is strong, then we can make the right decisions. He will give us peace and allow us to recover from our grief of losing a loved one or a friend or a family member. By having faith in Him, we will become a new person inside out. He is the key to everything in life, so we should turn to him. After all, He is the Carpenter of the Universe. The tragedy is part of our lives, and sorrow is a natural emotion. These times are part of our lives and will happen to either of us one time or the other. The fact of the matter is life still goes on. As long as you have faith in our Lord and Savior Jesus Christ, He will purify our heart and soul and keep us relaxed even in times of grief and distress. These are all transitions that we need to tackle, and we always need to prepare ourselves emotionally and mentally for them because they are bound to happen. People come and go, and one day all of us will leave this Earth too. The only way our souls will ever rest in peace is if we have continuously and constantly kept in touch with our Lord and Savior Jesus Christ all our lives and walked His path. This will enable us to live in peace and die in peace as well. We should be mindful of the fact that our faith gives us eternal salvation, and if our loved ones who left us walked His path, their souls would remain pure and peaceful too in death. We need to constantly remind us of this fact. We need to work very hard, and the transitions will be testing times for all of us.

These are the times we will need to prepare for so that when they happen, we're ready for them. Faith is quite powerful. As it can move mountains, it can also grant the believer peace, especially at stressful times.

Billy Joel once sang, "Life is a series of hellos and goodbyes," and it is quite true. The chorus of the song in which the line is taken from, Say Goodbye to Hollywood, is quite moving and makes sense here very much. The chorus goes as follows:

Moving on is a chance that you take every time

You try to stay together

Say a word out of line, and you find

That the friends you had are gone

Forever, forever

So many faces in and out of my life

Some will last, some will just be now and then

Life is a series of hellos and goodbyes

Transitions and transformations are a part of our lives because they present a series of changes in our lives. This because change, as stated above, is also the only constant in life. We need to be mindful of transitions and transformations in our life. Since change is honestly the only constant in life, we need to embrace it and not fear it. We grow from infants to teenagers to adults. We go through school, college, maybe even grad school, and eventually become professionals. We go through different phases, from adolescence to marriage and parenthood. These are all transitional phases. As much as some of us may deny this, we are always in a state of transition. Our lives are built in such a way that transitions will automatically happen without asking or expecting them. We need to be mindful of times when we are in the middle of these transitions. We need to constantly re-establish and strengthen our bond with God through all our trials and tribulations. As we experience change and transformations, we hope to grow even closer to God as it is He who we seek guidance from in such times. As we grow older and gain more responsibilities, we look up to God to guide us all the way and help us be prepared for the transitions and transformations in our life. The first step is to recognize when we're in that state of transformation and transition and realize what that entails. Once that's discovered, it's a lot easier to manage it because of a few things. First of all, we've already had a strong connection with Christ. Secondly, we realize it's either His way of testing us or just our lives normally transforming as they should. Finally, it shows us that our faith in Christ is so strong that we can handle any transformation with ease. It also ensures that we turn to Christ for all our problems because, after all, He is our Savior. It's a constant reminder for us to see who is in control of our lives and why it's important to keep the spiritual bond always strong.

Some transitions are easy, and some are tough. It is because, at each time, we look to God because these are from him. By putting faith in Him, we lift the burden off ourselves because He would only want the best for us. By believing in Him, we are already saved. This is why it's even more important to not get disheartened during some transitions that look unwelcoming from the get-go. These are just different ways to test our faith, and life is always full of these ever since the day we're born, and these will continue until the day we depart from this world. After all, we have blessed with everlasting life thanks to our faith in Christ. Keeping that in mind, we should take every transition, transformation, and turning points as signs from Christ. Even if the transitions bring about challenges, its times like these that you learn and discover more about yourself. This voyage of self-discovery makes you realize unrealized potentials. You break free from the limitations you've set yourself with. You realize that when you establish faith and keep that connection strong, then anything is possible.

Our lives have transformed with technology. Our society and economy have become more consumerist than it ever was before. Communication has never been easier between one or more persons. Thanks to the internet, our lives have definitely become easier. To meet the demands of the current economy and our new lifestyles, we become very consumed with our careers and extra-curricular. Where do we find time for faith? Do we lock faith up in a Church and just open the key on the Sunday sermons? Or do we lock faith up in our hearts and turn to it only in times of need? No matter how far technology advances and signs of progress, our faith should never take a hit. We should not be so consumed by the everyday lives that we forget God. It is He who made us, after all, and allowed us to create this incredible technology. We were gifted with the skills and knowledge to take technology far beyond than ever before. When the transitions and transformations happen, even in this day and age, we will turn to drugs, substance abuse, and alcohol if the transition is negative. I lost my job, and to me, that was more important. In truth, the job did pay for a lot of my needs, but losing it shouldn't be the end of the world. My faith in Christ helped me re-establish my relationship with him, even in such testing times. I realized there is nothing bigger than this association, and when you realize that losing a job doesn't feel like that much of a big deal. It only opens new doors because we have to trust Christ's plans for us. Once we know that, the possibilities are clearly endless. Christ loves us, and He only wants the best from us, so we should know that these transitions are times where we are only growing as a person.

Whenever a change happens in our life, we don't need to be disheartened or upset. We need to first tell ourselves we're not alone in this battle as Christ is with us. Then we need to re-establish our relationship with Him because it could be weaker. We need to exercise patience through this testing time, and then we will find a light at the end of the tunnel. That is our true calling. Once we hear that call and follow it, we'll realize we're in a much better place. So, that being said, we need to always follow His path no matter where life takes us. If we continue to walk in his path, then every issue that is big or small would be conquered without much trouble. Living life this way means that we can move along whatever life throws at us with our head held high because the Carpenter of the Universe is with us and will always be with us. We are blessed with the gift of eternal life, so what do we have to fear. I lost a job, but that was never the end but a new beginning. If we take life that way, we have absolutely nothing to fear. This is how life is meant to be lived as we have to reconnect with our faith during times of transitions and transformations. Transitions allow us to think about our life at certain points and re-evaluate ourselves. It allows us to decide how we should live our lives at those points and make crucial decisions. While it may seem scary, it really is not. Transitions teach us valuable life lessons and allow us to grow emotionally and spiritually; both kinds of growth are very important for our self-improvement. All of these transitions allow us to reconnect with our spiritual selves and, at the same time, re-establish our connection with our Lord and Savior Jesus Christ. That kind of connection is so important because that reconnection will help us make the best decisions we can make at the time because we took it with the confidence that our Lord and Savior Jesus Christ is giving His blessings. This allows us to become more self-assured and confident in handling the tough issues we see from time to time.

As explained in the chapter, transitions are a common part of our lives. Throughout our lives, we will see different situations that are life-changing. This could be the death of a loved one, marriage, children, new job, or anything that makes your life different. In this chapter, we saw how these life-changing events force us to make some tough decisions. Sometimes it's not easy to make those tough decisions, and I feel that it's the case almost all the time. Sound decision making comes from the fact that you're trusting an entity much bigger than yourself and what bigger entity than our

Lord and Savior Jesus Christ. A lot of times, transitions happen as we grow old. We go from high school to college, then graduate and find a job. We may become married, parents, and eventually, grandparents. Old age will hit us too if we live that long. Regardless, life will go on, and people will age, and that brings in another set of challenges for us. This is why it's important to realize the importance of transitions in our lives. With each transition as we grow older, we need to constantly stay in touch with our Lord and Savior Jesus Christ. Faith in Him smoothens the transitions that we experience in our lives. The idea here is to simply leave everything to Him and go with your gut. Make smart and calculated decisions in your life while keeping faith in Him, and you'll see yourself experience transitions just like it was a normal thing. Faith truly can move mountains, and you will realize it as your faith is strengthened and re-strengthened as you face transitions.

Transitions are a natural part of life, and we must learn to embrace them. These are all ways that God tests our faith, and we need to pass his tests. This is something we can learn from, and every transition is surely a learning experience. No matter what happens, good or bad, we can learn something from it. The next chapter will talk about spiritual evolution, and I must tell you that these transitions cause spiritual growth. It's these life experiences that shape us who we are today, so we don't need to be afraid. We need to place trust in our Heavenly Father that whatever happens, happens for the best. We need to know these things are very important. The first step most certainly is to trust God, and that is something we did explore in the first chapter. You can't place trust in anyone unless you believe in that person. Once we place our faith and trust in God, we need to understand the events that we experience in life. We need to understand how certain life experiences are important to us. We need to understand the fundamentals of our lives. God will show us the signs, and we need to follow them. Those signs will come to us naturally, and we will just know that those came from God. It is something that we need to very wary of. I am very confident that once your connection with God is established, you will welcome every change in life- good or bad. You will learn from them and grow. How that growth happens in something you will learn in the next chapter. You should never ever be afraid. Once you have placed your trust in God, there is nothing to worry about. He will pull you through as long as you stay firm in your beliefs. Transitions are completely normal, and every person on this planet will go through them. Once we are born, those transitions will take place. In every part of our lives, we will experience these, and not all of them will be good, and not all of them will be bad. For me, losing my job was not good, but it was a transition nonetheless. Had that not happened, I may not have come to write this book. There is a reason for everything to happen in your life. That's how life works. Once those transitions happen, just embrace them happily. I look back at those transitions positively. I don't get sad and depressed because I know they all come from our Lord and Savior, Jesus Christ. This is why you should embrace positive thinking because that's what God wants us to embrace as well.

We need to understand that spiritual growth doesn't happen without any transitions or turning points. We have a limited shelf life on Earth, and we have to do so much in that time we have. Our time consists of being born, growing up, learning the ropes, being an adult, being independent, working, getting married, having a family, and so on. Then in later years, our family gets further expanded, and health issues come knocking in. A lot of things happen, and we don't realize that there are natural transitions, and then there are those that are just thrust upon us. It's the latter that really helps us grow spiritually. A good way to understand growth is to look at the career of the late great pop superstar Michael Jackson. His musical evolution is legendary. As a child, he was part of his brothers' singing group Jackson 5, and managed by his father. As he grew older, he became the icon of the group. He became the group's biggest star. Over the years, as he grew, his talent grew. He became one of the promising artists among the Jackson 5. In the 1980s, Michael went solo and became a huge superstar in his own right selling millions of albums globally and setting world records. Michael's artistic evolution included his natural growth as a singer and a chain of events that made him the world's biggest-selling recording artist in the 1980s and 1990s. Michael was no longer just one of the Jackson 5 or The Jacksons as they were later known. He was a global superstar, and his influence and success have long continued after his death in the year 2009. Similarly to Michael, we also have grown in many ways. Now, here's a better way to explain my point. Coming back to Michael Jackson, he was immensely talented and developed into a phenomenal singer, musician, and dancer. He was just one of a kind. We could easily say that he was God-gifted because he most certainly was. All that immense talent came from God to Michael Jackson, and he kept on harnessing it. He worked on it night and day, and God gave him the success he deserved. Now, he had his share of challenges too. There were scandals and court cases.

His career dwindled in the late 1990s and his popularity, although high, wasn't even close to the level it was in the 1980s and early 1990s. Turning points and transitions happened in his life. There was talk about his eccentricities, and his face had changed. There was scrutiny on him about his plastic surgeries and the number of times he has done them. He would talk about his vitiligo skin condition. All the success in the world didn't prevent him from the different challenges he faced. God gave him incredible success but put him through various challenges, which we term as transitions and turning points. That's exactly how we need to look at our life too. We may not need to be God-gifted, but I have to say something here. We may not know, but each and every one of us has a certain kind of talent that we are very good at. It's that talent that helps us get the success we need and counter challenges. It could be one or multiple talents. All of these talents and gifts come from God. See, we're not just sent into the world without a plan. We all have been sent to different parts of the world and different economic conditions, and different backgrounds. All of these are decided by God, and that's how we live and grow up. The natural transitions happen, and that helps with growth, and there are many turning points or challenges that all of us have to face as well. These are the challenges, transitions, turning points that help our spiritual growth is. I will highlight the importance of being connected to God through all these times. It's very important that we go through these with complete faith in God, and He will help us through. If you haven't realized it yet, then you must. All of these are to help us connect with God. If God can bestow us with so many talents, gifts, and abilities, then he can even throw challenges in our path so we can use them to overcome them. Once we tap into God's power, then our gifts and talents become magnified, and then God pulls us through. Every success comes from him, and we need to recognize that. It's very important to also realize that every non-success and tragedy comes from Him too. That's why it's so important to stay connected to God at all times throughout life, whether there are good or bad times. We should never forget God because it is He who made us who we are, and He ensures our daily survival. This is why it's so important to work towards keeping that connection with Him strong. Challenges came in the way of our Lord and Savior Jesus Christ, but He persevered. He became an example for all mankind, and it is He who we must keep faith in for eternal salvation. We may be blessed with eternal salvation, but that doesn't mean life will be any easy. It just makes overcoming challenges easier because our Lord and Savior Jesus Christ is on our side. He is with us through all the pitfalls and turning points that life throws at us. Therefore, the connection with Him always needs to remain strong. We should never be afraid because all things, good and bad, come from our Heavenly Father. We will only grow spiritually if we stay true to Him and keep that connection strong all the time, no matter what happens to us in life. We need to remind ourselves at all times that we need to stay connected to Him at all times, and then great things will happen. We will become the superstar of our own lives because we are one with God!

So, all you need to do is reach out to God at all times and hold on to His rope because the stronger that grip is, the better you can survive the turning points and transitions. You should never be afraid because God will always be there for you, no matter what. You always need to look towards Him at all times, good or bad. This is the crux of the chapter because no matter where we are in life, the good or bad times don't last forever. We are always changing and evolving due to our transitions, turning points, and challenges. We have to know the most important goal is to please God. The most important thing to recognize and realize that God has the best interests at heart for us. We need to trust Him with everything, and things will be great. I can't tell you how relieved I feel because I now am very much connected to God at all times. It's so great that He is looking out for me, and I am ever so thankful to him. This is why you need to do the same, and you'll always feel happy and cheerful no matter what happens. Let the good times roll!

3

Expand, Evolve, and Expose

Expand and extend yourself to effectively fulfill purpose."

— Sunday Adelaja

"So he went with them. And when they came to the Jordan, they cut down trees." — II Kings 6:3

Life is a journey of learning and growing. The more we grow, the more we learn about ourselves as people. The more we learn about our purpose in life. As Christians, we have dedicated our lives to walk the path of Christ and spread His love on our planet and establish His kingdom. Growth is a lifelong process, and as we grow, we connect even closer to Christ. Change is the only constant in life, and growth is a process of change. As we grow older and wiser, we expand our horizons, and, in those horizons, we find God each and every time.

We see Christ's work in our lives. We will also see that we will change for the better and will impact the lives of those around us positively as well. It will then result in a chain reaction in which those same people will be spread a positive impact on their own communities, and it will become a circle of positivity going around. We will see more and more people turn towards our Lord and Savior Jesus Christ, and once they all put their faith in Him, the positivity will change our world for the better. We can save so many people from self-destruction this way.

The passage in II Kings 6: 3 shows an evolution. The prophet Elisha goes with the company of prophets to make a new dwelling for themselves, as their previous space was smaller. This was discussed in the previous chapter, and we move further on from that here. In order to get wood to build their new house, they came to 'the Jordan' and 'cut down trees.' The Jordan here most likely refers to the river Jordan. Here you see progress and change, and this is something we experience at every turn in our lives. We are evolving all the time ever since we are born. We are cutting down trees to make new houses. While it's all metaphorical, it makes sense here. When single people get married, they may choose to move to a newer place, which is larger than the one they're in. Going even deeper, we always have to reinvent ourselves as we grow and mature. Reinvention is a by-product of change, and as stated previously, that itself is the only constant in life. We have to change and reinvent ourselves so we can become better Christians and better human beings. In Jeremiah 29:11, it is said, 'For I know the plans I have for you,' declares the LORD, 'plans to prosper you and not to harm you, plans to give you hope and a future.'"

Reinventing oneself to become a better believer, a better Christian, and a better human being is earning Christ's love. He does love us unconditionally, but this is how we love him back by being people of moral character and a true believer in the fact that we have been saved and are destined for the afterlife. What the passage from

Kings II tells us that when we are confined to a smaller space, we must go out and cut down the trees to build a larger space. It's a transformation taking place. It's the idea that something big is planned for us, but we don't know it yet. We need to find that bigger space, and in order to find it and build it, we need to put our efforts into it. We've been told there is no such thing as a free lunch. Because we have been saved and destined for everlasting life, we have a responsibility upon other believers and non-believers. Someone paid a sacrifice for sins, and that was our Lord Jesus Christ. If He made such a huge sacrifice for us, then so can we.

An example of reinvention from the real world works here very well. Pop icon Madonna has been known to constantly reinvent herself, her style, her fashion sense, and even her music to stay in tune with the times. As a result, her music is still very popular, and her records still sell like hot cakes even today. Musically, Madonna grew as an artist and as a performer. Keeping this analogy in mind, we also need to grow and reinvent as

Christians. Sunday Adelaja's quote, Expand and extend yourself to effectively fulfill the purpose, explains my point quite well. We have to continuously grow and expand our thoughts and minds in order to fulfill our life's purpose, and for us Christians, it's walking in God's path. We need to find new areas of ourselves that do not suffer from spiritual dullness in order to be more mature. In Ephesians 4:22-24, it is said, "You were taught, with regard to your former way of life, to put off your old self, which is being corrupted by its deceitful desires; to be made new in the attitude of your minds; and to put on the new self, created to be like God in true righteousness and holiness." Here, our Lord and Savior Jesus Christ is saying we need to change as our old self was corrupted by deceitful desires. Our new self needs to be absolved and eradicated from sin, and that requires faith in Him. That faith, love, and bond we have with Him are what will change us.

Reinvention is a way to keep a check on your life and where you are at different points of your life. I explained

Madonna's example above as how people have reinvented themselves in the real world. Madonna would reinvent every few years or so to keep up with the times so she can stay relevant in the pop music business, which is always changing. People's tastes change over time, so she adapted her music and sound to fit the times while at the same time sticking to her pop and dance roots. There was always a little bit of old Madonna in every new album she put out despite them sounding different from each other. At the end of the day, you're still listening to a Madonna album. Similarly, one needs to readjust and reinvent themselves as they grow old and as different challenges come their way. Your life will change when you become a married person from a single person; you will have more responsibilities in life, you will need a better job to earn a higher income to support yourself and your spouse if he or she isn't working. When you become a father, your responsibilities will increase as well. These things are something to keep in mind. You will need to ask yourself these questions because you may be forced to reinvent even if you don't want to. As time goes by, you may need to educate yourself in different technologies, or you'll be behind the curve in the workplace or in life. Life is a process of learning. You have to learn, unlearn, and relearn things at different points of your life. You will need to do it because the world is always changing. New technologies are being invented each day, so you can only be "old school" for so long. We have to constantly update ourselves as well. When it comes to our faith, we need to keep a check on ourselves, too, and see if the connection with our Lord and Savior Jesus Christ is still active. We may need to change our life around in order to smoothen the connection too.

We face challenges on a daily basis. Whether its work, family, or even with friends, there are daily challenges depending on our interactions with them. Humans are social animals. At every point in our lives, we are presented with challenges. Perhaps, for men and women, a real challenge comes in the form of marriage. While it's supposed to be a happy union of two souls in the name of our Lord and Savior Jesus Christ, it comes with its own set of challenges. When you are living with another person, you and the other person has expectations of each other. Those expectations can't always be met; sometimes, we set unrealistic expectations, we can't meet them at all. In the previous chapter, we discussed transitions and turning points. In that sense, marriage can be deemed either a transition or a turning point. Men feel like their freedoms of the bachelor days are taken away while women expect to find a soulmate who will take care of their every need and give them love and affection. Men try to tackle the transition from being a bachelor to a loving husband and partner, and that transitions present challenges, both sides have to deal with those challenges properly. To tackle such challenges, reinvention is necessary. We would need to expand and evolve only, then the solutions can be exposed. Marriage is all about compromise, and that's why this holy matrimony can be such a challenging union. When expectations aren't met, then problems occur, and that results in conflicts and arguments. In order to protect ourselves from this situation, we need to be prepared to reinvent ourselves to tackle the problems. While it is easy to blame the other person, we must change ourselves first. We need to be role models for our spouses. This way, we can encourage them to evolve, expand, and reinvent themselves as we have. Our lives have become more demanding. We don't want to go down the untrodden path, the point of no return. I am speaking of divorce because if problems don't get resolved, they multiply, and eventually, the holy matrimony is no longer holy since it's over. These challenges need to be handled smartly and tactfully. As the marriage evolves, children can happen, and those pose their own sets of challenges. Even children have expectations. They need to be cared for and nurtured. They will have their own sets of needs, and those would need to be catered for. So, marriage definitely is a challenging experience. However, if handled well, it can be extremely rewarding. At the end of the day, building a family is a rewarding experience because you have a companion and loving children that become a huge part of your life just as you were for your parents. To raise a child from infancy is such a beautiful experience. Fatherhood and motherhood are two experiences that should be experienced at least once in your lives. The point I am making here is to make sure you all understand the natural transitions of men and women from single to married individuals, and then parents. Yes, if we're lucky, we can even become grandparents, but that's a bridge to cross when we get there. Those readers who are there would know very well what I mean. Even that itself is quite a beautiful and bountiful experience. When we are going through these transitions and natural evolutions, we will need to reinvent ourselves. We need to do that the right way, and that's where we need to look towards our Lord and Savior, Jesus Christ, for guidance. Once we strengthen the rope with Him and walk in His path and light, then we can handle these transitions well and reinvent ourselves accordingly. We can save ourselves from conflicts, arguments, and, most importantly, divorce. We can be better partners, companions, and spouses. No matter what issue we face, we can face with our spouse together as one unit united in the name of our Lord and Savior Jesus Christ. Our strength of faith will keep us together forever, and the marriage will survive the test of time. It's so important to realize that it is only faith in Him that will get us through these challenges effectively. We will be able to reinvent ourselves the right way and handle any situations thrown our way. Marriage is a privilege, responsibility, and duty, and while it comes with its set of challenges, love, care, and affection can solve anything. It is important to realize that it requires strength of character above everything, and that comes with faith in our Lord and Savior Jesus Christ. As we evolve, expand, and reinvent ourselves, whatever issue or problem gets exposed, any kind of spiritual dullness, we can rediscover our edge and keep our marriages healthy and happy. All of this can be achieved by loving and staying connected to our Lord and Savior, Jesus Christ, at all times.

As our lives become more and more demanding, we may not have time for spirituality, but that is something we will need to adjust on. It's an evolutionary process. You may have to become reborn again and again to be a better Christian and a human being. These things are extremely important to understand. You have to reinvent and evolve, and you have to make sure the others who have an impact on you and vice versa also do the same. It is imperative because you and those others who you impact and vice versa will have a positive effect on each other. Positive changes rub on others the right way, and those positive changes then encourage more positivity. This way, an entire circle of positivity can be achieved. When we are good Christians, we automatically become better human beings. We can then create positivity around us, and that will last long after we are gone. We can set an example for our future generations to follow. As stated in this book a few times, faith can move mountains. It clearly can make a huge difference because it is our faith in our Lord and Savior Jesus Christ that makes us do positive things. We can reinvent ourselves in a much positive manner so we can have a long-lasting effect on our families and the societies and communities we live in. It is, in fact, our responsibility to bring about positive changes in not just ourselves, the others that we are related to, and those who live with us. Change starts from within, and then it's transferred to others. While the sooner we realize how important it is to reinvent ourselves positively, the better it is for us in the long run. However, it's never too late to make a change.

While Madonna was reinventing herself and her music to please the masses of music fans, we need to do the same but not for the masses. We need to do it to please the Carpenter of the Universe, who has taken care of us since we were born and has guided us throughout our life till our last breath. It is very important we evolve as good Christians and good human beings at the same time. The process goes hand in hand.

I have stressed throughout this book how important it is to keep that connection with our Lord and Savior

Jesus Christ alive and have discussed different ways to do it. It is important to do not just that but also walk His path. Through that path, we will face several challenges, and we need to evolve and reinvent each time to face those challenges so that connection is never lost. You do realize that our lives and even those of our loved ones are temporary, but He will always be here, He will remain while everyone around us and even us too will be going into the dirt, where we came from. This is why He is the one we must always please, so evolution and reinvention are extremely important. This process may seem long and hard because our lives will get harder as we grow. We may forget our responsibilities toward our Lord and Savior Jesus Christ because it's easier for us to remember our responsibilities to our life, our work, and our families and friends. While those are extremely important, we must not forget our responsibilities to the one being who created us and breathed life into us.

Evolution and reinvention should always be for the better because there would be no other reason to do so

When life changes for us, we need to change. We need to adapt, overcome, and persevere whatever challenges life presents for us. We may be wondering that if reinvention is important, how we make that change happen. It's important to know that our Lord and Savior Jesus Christ is the key to our reinvention. We need to keep that connection active, so we continue to have a strong relationship with Him. This is the only way we can reinvent and evolve for the better. He is the key to which our change will take place. We need to change for Him at all times, and for that, we need to look towards him for guidance at all times. That guidance is important. See, in life, we do look for advice from others. It could be our parents, spouse, friends, or work colleagues. There can be good advisors and bad advisors. We need to choose those advisors carefully. This is because if we take the wrong advice, we will only harm ourselves, and if we take the right advice, we will benefit ourselves. Sometimes, it's hard to know who one can trust and can't. It's hard to know who is truly sincere, honest, and genuine with you. These things are extremely important to always keep in mind. You need to know that person inside out and vice versa. We may be confused even after speaking to any of our advising friends or family. What I am trying to explain here is that there is an even better advisor we can all talk to. He is the one who will always be the most sincere, genuine, and honest with us. If you don't know who I am talking of, he is none other than our Lord and Savior Jesus Christ. He knows us better than anyone else, and that includes our parents, our best friends, our spouses, and anyone else. He is the one we should always trust. His advice and guidance will only help us and never hurt us. So, when we are looking for a change, we need to look towards Him, and not only that, follow His guidance and advice. If we want to become better Christians and better human beings,

He is the key. He is the one being that through the right change will happen in our lives. This is why we will be walking in His path because we want to please Him. Walking in His path will present challenges, and that's where our spiritual evolution, growth, and reinvention will come from. Change starts from within, and that is something we need to recognize and realize sooner than later. That change needs to be a complete change. We need to completely reinvent and revamp ourselves spiritually as we walk the path of our Lord and Savior Jesus Christ. It needs to be a spiritual rebirth ac time. As we have recognized change being the only constant in our life, we need to embrace it, especially if that is a spiritual rebirth. We need to first cleanse ourselves inside out to become a completely new person spiritually. We need to do a self-analysis of where we lack, especially those spiritually dry areas, and then acknowledge those. Then, we can start the process of spiritual reinvention from there. We will slowly shed our old spiritual selves and become reborn in Christ. We will feel so much better, and our change will be felt by others around us, and they will see how happy and relaxed we are because we know who the key to that change is. Our change will enlighten others around us to go through a process of spiritual reinvention and growth themselves because they also want to be in that light- the light of our Lord and Savior Jesus Christ. This is the way we can spread His love and grace all around us. See, we can impact and change so many people's lives this way. This is the beauty of Christ's grace. First, we need to change ourselves so we can impact others positively with our change, and then they can change themselves. Therefore, those people will change others around them, and the collective change will only bring peace in all our lives. We should never be afraid to embrace change. Change is beautiful, and especially if it's inspired by our Lord and Savior Jesus Christ, then there is nothing better than that. Our reinvention and change will allow us to tackle life's problems in a much better manner, and we can continue to be a positive influence on our family, our friends, and others around us, such as work colleagues, neighbors, and so on. Such change and growth are beautiful, and I can say from my own experience that it is. I want to encourage each and every one of you to reinvent and change yourselves spiritually every so often so your connection with our Lord and Savior Jesus Christ stays strong at all times.

Our Lord and Savior Jesus Christ uses growth in one area to uncover dullness in another. This way, as you grow on one side of your personality, you keep uncovering dullness in other areas. This way, you realize which areas of dullness need to be sharpened. You need to realize which areas of yourself and your life that are spiritually dull and need sharpening. It could be different ways to give back to your society. This requires deep self-analysis, and then you'll see where you need to grow and mature. Such deep thought will result in deeply spiritual evolution. See, we are always evolving since the day we were born. We develop different traits as we grow, and that gives us a personality. It's important to know that evolution needs to be in the right direction. We can't evolve in the wrong direction. The more we know about each other and where we lack spiritually, we can evolve in those areas. It's this process that, despite taking time, makes us into better Christians and human beings. Spiritual evolution is a natural phenomenon, and it happens the more we look into ourselves and work on the areas that are spiritually dull. It's about examining yourself completely and improving ourselves. Evolution leads to self-improvement. The important thing we need to know is that there is always room for improvement. Its graduate, but improvement always needs to be in motion; it also needs to happen every time. So we need to constantly work on ourselves and improve ourselves, and we will be guided by our Lord and Savior Jesus Christ. It's very important for us to do this, and it has to be an active process. Every single day, we need to work on ourselves. Because it's the baby steps that we make that lead to the bigger steps and changes in our life. We don't need to be afraid of change because we are changing every day without even knowing about them. Once our faith in our Lord and Savior, Jesus Christ, is so strong, then things can happen for us. The changes will become more evident, and it will be a great feeling. When you walk in the path of our Lord and Savior Jesus Christ, you will feel the change on a daily basis. You will become a much better person to yourself and others around you. You will then inspire others to make that change in themselves based on you. Spiritual evolution is a truly beautiful feeling, and we should always keep that process going. Most of us who were not Christians before, most who did not believe in the power and love of our Lord and Savior Jesus Christ, were different. We chose to change our lives and evolve into God-fearing Christians and human beings. It was the faith in our Lord and Savior Jesus Christ that changed us, that allowed us to evolve into better human beings. We began walking in his path and were blessed by his light and changed. We saw so many things in our life change. The way we interacted with people, the way we acted on things, and how we handled situations all changed. The way we reacted to situations changed too. We began to think positive and positive thinking is a great virtue. We became more loving and forgiving. We became more down to earth. We began to love our neighbors and respect our parents more than we did. We encouraged positive thinking in our children. We taught them about the love of our Lord and Savior, Jesus Christ. We learned so much about ourselves that we never knew before. So much of the good stuff inside us was hidden, and we nurtured that. We became a good influence and inspiration to people around us. We made love our mantra and spread it to the entire humanity in the name of our Lord and Savior, Jesus Christ. The biggest evolution in our life comes when we accept Jesus Christ as our Lord and Savior, and then everything else starts from there. Every other change begins from there. The feeling of being blessed with eternal salvation is a beautiful feeling. Only those of us who have experienced know that, and it's truly an amazing feeling because we are now able to walk in the path of our Lord and Savior Jesus Christ. In such a state, all our problems become smaller, and we're able to tackle them head-on. We become stronger and confident individuals who fear no one except our Lord and Savior, Jesus Christ. We know that we have His back, so every problem becomes no problem, and solutions just appear. This is because we take every decision knowing that we have His love, blessings, and backing. We could never be afraid of any other human being at all, Christian or not. I feel one of the best traits one possesses as a believer in Christ is forgiveness. Forgiveness is a key virtue, and to forgive others helps to sharpen those dull areas that we have talked about in this book so much. We learn to appreciate the goodness in others as well. Forgiveness is very hard, but to be honest, it isn't hard for our Lord and Savior Jesus Christ at all. It is very easy because he has forgiven us and taken the burden of all our sins, then why can't we forgive our fellow brothers and sisters. Why can't we be more giving human beings? Forgiveness will get us closer to our Lord and Savior Jesus Christ a lot more than keeping a grudge. It will also inspire others to do good and start believing in the love of our Lord and Savior, Jesus Christ. It will turn us towards Him more and others as well. To be a Christian is a huge responsibility, and we can uphold it by walking the path of our Lord and Savior Jesus Christ. It's faith in Him that gives us peace in hearts and minds, and that transcends to others around us. In Matthew 5:39-40, it is said, "But I tell you, do not resist an evil person. If anyone slaps you on the right cheek, turn to them the other cheek also." This is the Word of our Lord and Savior Jesus Christ that this is how we need to be forgiving and tolerant towards those who antagonize us. If someone slaps us on one cheek, we should let him slap the other one. This will show the other person that we care for him, and we love him because our Lord and Savior Jesus Christ commands us to love him and every other human being. It pleases him, so it pleases us to do the same. It makes us humble because life is too short to keep grudges. Jesus Christ is love, and we must always spread that message of love everywhere we go. We will constantly feel spiritually fulfilled. We will feel so much more at peace than we have ever felt in our lives. When we love others the same way our Lord and Savior Jesus Christ loves us, that's a spiritual evolution on a whole new level. Unfortunately, tolerance isn't so prevalent in our society, and people would rather take revenge on others other than forgiving them. Revenge is never the answer. By forgiving and displaying tolerance, you don't only please our Lord and Savior Jesus Christ, you turn those who hurt you towards him. You help them see the light of Jesus Christ. When they would ask you why you forgive them, you can tell them that you are only following the commands of our Lord and Savior Jesus Christ, and if it pleases Him, it pleases us. If not, then, but sometime later, that person will turn to our Lord and Savior Jesus Christ and become a better person and human being. You would not only evolve yourself but will also help others in their spiritual evolution. They will thank you for showing them the Light. We are duty-bound by our Lord and Savior to do this. Spiritual evolutions don't mean only that you have to change yourself, but you also have to inspire others to seek changes in themselves. It would be the best gift you can give to others around you. By sharing and spreading the love of our Lord and Savior Jesus Christ, you are doing mankind a huge favor. It will fill our spiritually dark areas with everlasting light, and that light will shine in others around us too, and they will see their own spiritually dark areas become illuminated with the love of our Lord and Savior Jesus Christ. Once we start thinking on that higher level, we never go back. We would have just elevated ourselves spiritually so much that others will see that and seek inspiration from us and make efforts to get to that high level too. It's very important that our peers feel as enlightened as we do when they evolve. If they need guidance, guide them because someone guided you too probably. It is true that our Lord and Savior Jesus Christ is our guide and will make sure to show us through signs about how we should spiritually evolve. Sometimes, we get signs from others who have been through this kind of spiritual evolution. We should be inspired and inspire others too. We, humans, are social animals, so we need to learn from others' successes and failures. That's the beauty of our lives because the signs are present, among others, and we should seek them. It is upon us to seek guidance, guide others, and enable them to guide others as well. At the end of the day, we are doing the work of our Heavenly Father.

At every step of our spiritual growth, God never leaves us. Desiring Christ quotes this verse from the Bible that illustrates my point: "The Lord your God is in your midst, a mighty one who will save; he will rejoice over you with gladness; he will quiet you by his love; he will exult over you with loud singing." (Zephaniah 3:17) The same website further states, "The beauty of Christ's love is that it survives spiritual dry times. Don't let the lie sink into your mind that spiritual dryness indicates that Christ has gotten over you, or that he's tired of working with you. Far from it." The idea here is that Christ doesn't abandon you. You may be at times in your life where you feel spiritually dry, it is when you seek Christ, and you realize He's always been there. He's just waiting for you to acknowledge His place in your life. You need to understand that you can evolve and change for the better. You need to know that our Lord and Savior Jesus Christ will always be there, so never lose hope. Once you seek Him out, whether through prayer or being inspired by others, you will see a natural evolution taking place in you. You may not realize it, but you will see it happening, and you will feel very elevated. You will feel spiritually lifted, and that is such a beautiful feeling. I have been through this evolution, and I can tell you it's amazing. That being said, my evolution hasn't stopped.

You see, change is the only constant in life. So we will always evolve spiritually in one way or the other. Whenever we feel spiritually dry, that's the time to evolve. It doesn't just have to happen at one time in our lives but can happen multiple times over the course of our lives. You'll just know when you need to evolve. As explained in this chapter, situations in your life may force you to do so, or you may find the eagerness inside you to evolve. I would urge and encourage you to welcome that change wholeheartedly because that comes from our Lord and Savior Jesus Christ. All you need to do is look within your heart and look out for signs. You will know when they are present. There's no set time. They will happen instantaneously, and you'll know it's the time to evolve. We have mentioned Madonna in this chapter. For example, as a pop musician, she knew that times were changing, and so was people's taste in pop music. She adapted her musical style to those changes and was successful. Similarly, we will see the signs in our spiritual life. I must admit that my job loss was perhaps the sign that made me evolve. It was what I needed to transform myself.

Christ works on those of us more that have lost the edge and those of us that have lost our way. He creates us, so why would He abandon us? The idea here is at any stage in life you feel spiritually low, you'll need to look towards Christ and realize that He can fill the emptiness in your heart and soul. In Psalms 121:1 to 121:8, it is said, "I lift up my eyes to the mountains— where does my help come from? My help comes from the LORD, the Maker of heaven and earth. He will not let your foot slip— he who watches over you will not slumber; indeed, he who watches over Israel will neither slumber nor sleep. The LORD watches over you— the LORD is your shade at your right hand; the sun will not harm you by day, nor the moon by night. The LORD will keep you from all harm— he will watch over your life; the LORD will watch over your coming and going both now and forevermore." This is why we must never lose faith in our Lord and Savior, Jesus Christ. He is watching over us and will always guide us as long as we are connected to Him. We need to trust in Him that whatever decisions we make in His name will be the best for us. We will eventually learn that the outcome was the best for us when it happens. We will learn and enjoy the power we get from the knowledge we have gained from our faith in the Carpenter of the Universe.

I realized this when I lost my job. I knew I had to grow and mature to realize there's a force much stronger than all of us that controls the universe and controls us. He knows of our thoughts and emotions better than we know ourselves, and it is He who we need to seek guidance from and look towards when times are tough. The more we grow and discover about ourselves, the more we will see God's work in our lives, and we will use His love to inspire others so they can share His love and His grace with the rest of the world. I realized later that losing my job wasn't the end for me; it was just the beginning. It was a time for change and reinvention. It allowed me to look at my life and see where it was heading and why it came to this point. It was a time for me to pause my life for some time to see if I am heading in the right direction. Perhaps, a change was needed, and the opportunity came for me to make that change. We have heard that with every crisis, there is an opportunity, and my crisis gave me that opportunity. Like anyone else, I didn't realize it until later that it was a calling from our Lord and Savior Jesus Christ, and it was my time to change. It wasn't just a direction change but a complete cleansing of my soul. That cleansing was inside and outside, so I could become a completely new individual, in a sense, I would be considered reborn. At the time I lost my job, I was tense. Over time, I realized how it was a blessing in disguise when I was able to evolve spiritually. For me, it was only just the beginning. In the future, if such circumstances repeat, I will know exactly how to react. This entire episode was perhaps the best thing that happened to me. To be completely honest, I wouldn't wish anyone a job loss. All I am saying is that you need to look at such situations positively and not negatively. You need to know that our

Lord and Savior Jesus Christ will never let us down. During our transitions, He will look after us as long as we maintain our connection with Him. Positive thinking is important here. It's normal to feel upset, but when you know that our Lord and Savior Jesus Christ is there, what is there to fear?

That is such an exciting feeling as you look at life with a new lens. The same old lens you wore before on your eyes has become tainted, so a new lens is needed. This new coat of paint will help you find solutions to problems and become a better individual. That's what spiritual evolution is all about. You grow, you mature, you learn, and discover solutions to new problems. You can look at the spiritual evolution as a lifelong rehab that's completely free of cost. It keeps us free of sin and allows us to walk the path of our Lord and Savior, Jesus Christ.

As we grow and mature, we'll find ourselves going through periods of spiritual dryness. We may ask ourselves why this is happening, and we may not always find the answers. The more we relentlessly pursue God and make efforts to be close to him, we find ourselves struggling. The idea here is quite simple, really, and nothing to worry about. It is not that God is upset with us, or we have committed sins. The idea is that we shouldn't be taking Him for granted. We can't expect all our prayers to be answered without us truly seeking him. From time to time, God will test our faith, and then He will provide. So, if there are areas in which there is spiritual dryness, we must uncover them to find out where we lack faith. It will take time and a lot of patience, but eventually, we will be rewarded with spiritual sharpness. Those tests are essentially the time where we have to reinvent ourselves so we can become better Christians and human beings. These tests in our lives are signs from our Lord and Savior, Jesus Christ, that change is needed. This is when we need to act and do a self-evaluation of ourselves, our personalities, and our lives. Then, we must go through that process so we can tackle the challenges presented in front of us and conquer them. In many ways, when our connection with our Lord and Savior Jesus Christ grows weaker, that is also when these tests and challenges happen. We need to keep this in mind at all times in our lives and make sure that we are constantly reinventing ourselves for Him. Let me give you one great example. See, you want to always impress your spouse or your significant other or even your parents. Over the course of time, you will change things about you for their happiness. What I am explaining here is that we need to continuously evolve so we can please our Lord and Savior Jesus Christ. Pleasing Him is the best thing we can do as Christians, and it's so spiritually rewarding, it's unbelievable. You'll see your entire life will be about pleasing Him. You will do everything to make sure that the connection stays strong. So you will feel like a new person every so often, which is truly amazing.

This chapter essentially speaks about self-discovery, and it involves looking at yourself and your life deeply and carefully. Once you have conducted this analysis, you will find areas of spiritual dryness, and when you have figured those out, you can work on those areas. The best way to do is to re-strengthen and re-establish our connection with our Lord and Savior Jesus Christ. Once that connection is established, you need to hold on to the rope of your Lord and Savior Jesus Christ and simply walk in His path. Once you're walking in His path, you will be able to sharpen those areas of spiritual dryness with some effort. It will take time and effort, but you should know that the Carpenter of the Universe is going to guide you all the way. If He has created you, He knows better which areas you lack spiritual sharpness in, and faith in Him will help you uncover those areas. Once those areas are uncovered, you need to simply sharpen those areas. Once those areas are sharpened, you will discover a newer and deeper connection with your Lord and Savior Jesus Christ. This is a continuous process, and you need to do it every so often. The thing is we are born sinners, and we can be spiritually weak at times. It is our responsibility to make sure we are evaluating ourselves at all times. This self-evaluation is a lifelong process. The reason is that we face so many issues in our lives growing up, and at different stages of our lives, we have to face different challenges. All these challenges, hurdles, obstacles, and life's curveballs are life-changing. So many things can happen through these, and I can tell you from experience how they can change a person. For me, my job loss was a life-changing experience, and that experience was very enlightening; I like to keep drawing on that experience in this book because it was such an impactful and significant event for me in my life that it had changed me. It forced me to think about my life and where it was going, and it encouraged me to evaluate myself and my faith. I knew changes had to be made in my life, and those had to be positive changes. The point I am trying to make here is we need to check ourselves at all times. Life is very unpredictable, and that unpredictability is a beautiful thing, and I am saying that with utmost sincerity. Self-evaluation is important. As was the case with my job loss, I really had to decide for myself what kind of future I want for myself with this and how that future will impact my family and myself foremost and then others around me. It also encouraged me to reach out to our Lord and Savior Jesus Christ and burdening all my problems and issues to Him, so I can be rightfully guided. That is exactly what we all need to do, and this is what forms the crux of this chapter. It is my hope that by reading this, you all are also constantly and regularly evaluating yourselves, Always make sure to stay tuned to our Lord and Savior Jesus Christ, because it is only He who can guide us to the right path. So, it is my sincere advice to keep faith in Him at all times, and by re-evaluating yourself at all times, you're doing yourself a great favor. Not only that, but you also please our Lord and Savior Jesus Christ. That itself can be a strong motivator for your spiritual evolution. You can find those spiritually dull areas within yourself and your life and focus on those like I did. I wish you the best in honing on those spiritually dull areas and sharpening them so you can win back your edge!

Spiritual evolution is a natural process. It takes time, faith, and hard work to evolve spiritually. However, it's not just done solo. The only way to spiritual evolution is via our Lord and Savior Jesus Christ. Make no mistake. You can't achieve a single ounce of spiritual evolution by yourself. The only way to spiritual redemption and salvation is through our Lord and Savior Jesus Christ. It's a lifelong process, so you can't stop once you set foot on that path. One should embrace evolution. I've given examples of pop star Madonna who embraced musical evolution, which resulted in most of her albums sounding differently from the one before. It showed an evolutionary process. The sound was getting mature and diverse. Similarly, we need our Lord and Savior Jesus Christ to achieve the same kind of evolution, but it's not musical; it's spiritual. We need to reach inside ourselves and find God there. Once that connection is established, then it's as easy as 1, 2, and 3. When we seek to grow spiritually, we need to reach out to our Heavenly Father because He is the only one who can give us everlasting salvation. If that connection isn't present, then there is nothing you can do about it. You can't grow spiritually at all. Spiritual evolution is very exciting once you embrace it. You can do it. God is waiting for us to connect with Him, so we shouldn't hesitate. Once we evolve, we can expose all the areas where we lack spiritually, and then we can cover those areas with the help of our Lord and Savior, Jesus Christ. The first step is to connect with Him and keep that connection so strong that evolution takes place. It is then you will see the changes taking place in your life. That's the key, and the holder of the key is none other than our Lord and Savior Jesus Christ.

4

Plan, Prepare, & Perform

"Opportunity does not waste time with those who are unprepared." — Idowu Koyenikan

"But as one was cutting down a tree, the iron ax head fell into the water, and he cried out and said, Alas, master! For it was borrowed" — II Kings 6:5

Preparation and planning are essential in the process of regaining your spiritual edge because unpreparedness is an indication of spiritual immaturity. It presumes that our future does not hold important value. Value is ascribed to elements within our life that we deem important enough to invest time and effort. However, when we fail to plan, we are leaving our lives to become subject to the harsh dictates of others and circumstances and not in the hand of Christ. To illustrate, the passage of scripture that highlights this chapter reveals that while the man thought it important to begin to build in the new location that was discovered by the company of prophets, his lack of testing of the borrowed axehead uncovers a spiritual reality that all too often defines our lives as we hurriedly embrace new opportunities without planning. Thus, not only did the man lose the ax-head physically, but the spiritual reality of losing "our heads" spiritually could be comprehended within this passage. How often do we lose our heads in frustration because of a lack of preparation and planning? Thus, it important as new opportunities arise within our lives that we do not rush without planning and preparing for our futures. Second, the fact that the ax-head was borrowed and not his own suggests that many times within our lives, we are irresponsible with the instruments of others when new opportunities occur within our lives. Because he has to borrow another man's instrument in times of transitions displays another element of unpreparedness within his life. Too many times, what often looks like misfortune, is nothing more than a lack of preparation when analyzed.

Let me explain preparation in a different way, so it's easy to understand. When countries "prepare" to go to war, their commanders plan military strategies. The battle itself doesn't last long, but the preparation takes a lot of time and planning. Strategies are discussed, and plans are exchanged. Some are discarded while some are accepted. Both sides go through this several times, and then they proceed to battle. It is quite clear that preparation is key. While this is an example of a military strategy, it can be applied to so many facets of our life. For example, when you're preparing for job interviews or college examinations or even the SATs, you prepare in advance. If it's an exam, you prepare by learning, understanding, and absorbing the material. Then you do the trial tests and exams, and you keep doing them until you reach your desired score. Then you go to the exam and give your best. When it's a job interview, you research the company, the job you applied for, the board of directors, and other things necessary to impress the interviewer. You pick out your best formal dress and get ready to rock and roll. Once you feel suitably prepared, you go into the interview dressed to impress. We can even apply this to wedding preparations. You need to prepare months in advance for weddings. This includes booking the venue, decorations, food, catering, bridal dresses, groom suits, and so on. You prepare invitation cards and make sure everything is ready before the big day. In every case I have talked about, preparation is key. It is so important to be prepared. There is no harm in being overprepared, but one should never be underprepared. In the previous chapter, we talked about spiritual evolution. When there are gaps between our evolution, we need to be prepared for our next spiritual evolution. That's where preparation and planning come in. One can argue that we are always spiritually evolving when connected to our Lord and Savior, Jesus Christ, at all times. However, in real life, it is not possible to always be connected. We strive to keep that connection strong, but in those gaps, we should be suitably prepared.

We all have heard the sayings, 'strike when the iron is hot,' 'opportunity knocks only once,' 'time waits for no man,' and so on. All these sayings stress on preparedness. You should be prepared to jump on the opportunity when you find it. These are important things to consider when availing opportunities. You don't want to be the one regretting that you missed the bus. Timing is everything. In life, we are greeted with opportunities all the time, but we need to be prepared for them. The saying above by Idowu Koyenikan, "Opportunity does not waste time with those who are unprepared," is very true. Preparedness is extremely important. It's the same with our relationship with God. God provides us opportunities in life to get closer to Him, and it is for us to realize and recognize those opportunities. We've talked about transformations and transitions previously, and the idea here is we need to be prepared for these turning points in our lives, and then we can grab hold of the opportunity as it comes. The more we are prepared, the better we will be able to adapt to different situations in life. We will find new ways to keep our connection alive and kicking with our Lord and Savior, Jesus Christ. Our ultimate goal is to make sure there is never any lapse in connection. However, our real lives present challenges, so we need to be prepared mentally and spiritually for them. The idea I am trying to explain in this chapter is that there are three things to consider when it comes to being prepared. Let's call them extensions of preparation. The first is to be prepared. That involves a lot of planning, as explained above. Finally, when all is said and done, you need to perform and execute. An example that comes to mind is a team and individual sports. For every match, the sportsman prepares by training in the gym, on the courts or the field, and then makes sure he is ready to face his opponent. In team sports such as soccer, the teams regularly prepare for matches and work rigorously to make sure they perform on matchday. When match day arrives, they have to put it all out there on the field and give it their best. The analogies we can come up with are infinite. Whether it's a sports game or a musical performance, anything that requires preparation, the three elements I speak of are extremely important. This is how your probability and chances of success will be high.

Here, the saying "in every crisis, there is an opportunity' makes sense. The idea here is, at times of adversity, the opportunity is right there in front of us to get close to God. Adversity is an opportunity to either strengthen our ties with God by seeking his help or weakening it by losing hope in his help. For example, I lost my job, and I could have totally given up hope, but I used that opportunity in that transitional phase in my life to re-strengthen my relationship with God. I looked to Him for guidance, and eventually, He turned my life around. That's the power of faith, and it's very strong once you make that connection. Faith is a powerful healer, and I've been healed.

In the passage above from II Kings 6:5, "But as one was cutting down a tree, the iron ax head fell into the water, and he cried out and said, Alas, master! For it was borrowed," we see that one of the sons of the prophets lost the iron ax head as it went inside the water. He also says that it wasn't his. He couldn't afford an ax and had to borrow it. Here we see adversity. This is me at the time of losing my job, feeling that all hope is lost. How will I provide for my family? How will I live? Will I get another job? The son of the prophets also felt the same as in how will he now cut more wood and what about the iron ax head that's now submerged in water. He is concerned even about returning it to the person he borrowed from or somehow compensating him for the damages. These are all-natural concerns of any person in any sort of hurdle. These are times when you need to strengthen your bond and connection with God. Once your faith in Him is re-strengthened, then He will light the way.

Anthony Moore, writing for Medium, says, "If an opportunity passes through your fingers, or you get crossed over and forgotten, it's probably because you were unprepared." This is exactly the point being stressed in this chapter. This is something that applies to every person from all walks of life. Moore further says, "This is true for every one of our key areas in life. Relationships, career, finances, health, and success—amazing opportunities pass people by all the time because the individual was unprepared to seize it." That's the way we need to look at life and the opportunities that come our way. What stops us from being prepared? What hinders our readiness to strike when the iron is hot? Moore answers this way, "Maybe they hadn't learned enough yet. Maybe they keep getting passed over for their 'dream job' because they simply don't have the knowledge or skills to succeed yet." In practical life, this case holds true. We could simply be underqualified for a job or not have enough experience under our belt. This is why we would lose to job to others who would be considered more 'deserving candidates' than us for the job we are seeking employment for.

There could be another reason that we may have yet not considered. That's power. Moore uses the famous line from the Spider-Man comic books and films, "With great power comes great responsibility" in his article, and it also fits so well within our spectrum. This famous line was quoted by the character of Uncle Ben to Peter Parker. This became more meaningful to Peter as this was one of the last lines he would hear from his uncle prior to his eventual demise. His death at the hands of a criminal inspired Peter to become Spider-Man after he realized that his powers should be used for the good of mankind, starting with protecting the people of New York City. His power came with responsibility- the responsibility to protect those you love and the innocent who are powerless against ruthless thugs and criminals. Similarly, our faith comes with power, too, and we are also given responsibility too. Some of us may haven't realized that, yet Moore suggests that those of us have too much pride in our hearts to realize we aren't ready for that kind of responsibility. He says, "Most people actually couldn't handle the responsibility or power that would come with a sudden better station in life." It may not even be about being unable to realize, recognize, and handle the responsibility that 'great power' gives us. Moore says that perhaps some people are "just lazy. They haven't prepared or readied themselves to strike when the moment arrives." The last point is what I am trying to stress. We really need to be prepared to strike when the right opportunity arrives at our doorstep. We can't simply afford to be lazy. Opportunities don't come often, and we can very often miss the bus because we didn't act on the opportunity when it comes our way. You have to analyze the opportunities presented to you and weigh the pros and cons, and then make the right decision that you feel is best for you and your loved ones and those who depend on you. That could be your family and even friends to an extent. The best advice I can give you is here is that you shouldn't wait too long to weigh the pros and cons; otherwise, those opportunities will pass you by. Basically, what I mean to say is that you shouldn't waste too much time thinking about those opportunities. Once you have faith in our Lord and Savior Jesus Christ, He will guide you to the right path, and your faith will help you make the right decision for yourselves and your loved ones. You have to pray to Him, and you shall find the answers you seek. For example, after I lost my job, I would once again attack the job market to seek a better opportunity for myself and my loved ones. Within some time, I will get opportunities such as job offers, and those could be one or multiple. The time duration depends on how aggressive you are in looking for work and how strong your resume is, but you have to play the waiting game like everyone in this situation does. You have to analyze each offer properly and make sure it's the one you want. You need to weigh the pros and cons and then act quickly when it is time to make the decision. If you're stuck with multiple offers and are confused about what to do, you have a few options that you can look into. Firstly, you can choose from the current set of job offers if each pays more or less the same and offer similar benefits and are also in a similar field to the one you were in before and adds on to your experience. You don't know which one will be better as there's no way to be too sure. Sure, you can ask your friends and family for guidance or anyone in that industry or workplace for advice. If you can't find someone who offers good advice or a current or past employee of those places, then you have to go with your gut and what you feel is best. Obviously, it becomes a tough decision in the end. If you feel lost and even confused, you'll need guidance. The right guidance will come from our Lord and Savior, Jesus Christ. If we continue to hold on to his rope, we can make the right decisions at the right time. Going back to the job choice example, we have another choice. We can wait for better offers to come our way if none of the current options fit our requirements. At the same time, we need to know how long we can survive without a job in hand. If we can be comfortable, we can wait. Once again, you may find yourself confused, and you would require answers. All you need to do is hold steadfast to the rope of our Lord and Savior, Jesus Christ, and make the right decisions. As long as your faith is strong, you will never make a wrong decision in your life, and you will strike when the iron is hot. At the same time, you need to be responsible for all the decisions that you make in life. The Heavenly Father will guide you, but the decisions you make are your own. He will prepare you to make the right decisions, but ultimately the power is in your hands. Preparedness is key, so it is His guidance that makes us prepared for what's to come next in our lives, so we should always take heed.

See, God tests us at these precarious times so we can be prepared to yield the awesome power that makes us responsible. The power to walk in the path of God. It is to seek Him in times of transitions. Moore has pointed out above that we need to be ready. We can't be lazy, and we need to realize that we are indeed gifted with the everlasting life that belief in Jesus Christ as our Lord and Savior give us. This gift, this power, this is our responsibility to represent the Kingdom of God on Earth.

We need to be the friendly, neighbor Spider-Men of our own lives and our families, and our neighbors and other people around us. We need to do this for ourselves too. Once we realize and recognize the opportunity by being prepared for it, it will unravel itself, and we will be shown the path to success. We can be the heroes of our own lives once we realize that great power does come with great responsibility. That power comes from our Lord and Savior Jesus Christ, and our responsibility is to walk His path at every turn of our lives and to have complete trust and faith in Him. You must realize that knowledge is power, and power, in turn, is responsibility. We must learn how to use that power wisely at all times. One thing we must understand is that knowledge is power. And power is a responsibility. We need to prepare ourselves once we have that knowledge and guidance from our Lord and Savior, Jesus Christ. At the same time, we need to prepare others around us too. This way, they can benefit from our knowledge and guidance that we received from our Heavenly Father, and they could spread it to others as well. Knowledge and guidance are meant to be shared, and the more people have it, the more they could pass it on too. This way, we can spread the love of our Lord and Savior Jesus Christ to everyone around us.

Life is no bed of roses, and as the passage from II Kings 6: 5 shows us, even sons of prophets have been tested. A lot of the prophets, including Abraham, Moses, and Noah, have been tested, and it is in those times, they seized the opportunities to become close to God, and these were the ones already the closest to God. They were still tested and passed each and every obstacle with flying colors thanks to their undying love for God and their endless faith in His love and mercy. God tests those he loves because that's how we are able to re-strengthen our faith with Him. In the end, if we keep our faith in Him alive at every step, we will come on top each time. You can call it tough love that you would get from your parents growing up or from your bosses at work, or even sincere friends. All of these same people care for you and love you and always have your best interests in mind, so their tough love isn't meant to hurt you. It is their way of re-strengthening their bond with you so you can become a better person. Similarly, God loves us way more than our parents, our bosses, and our sincere friends. His love is boundless and infinite. We need to trust God the same way we trust our parents, bosses, and sincere friends. Trust is key because when you completely have faith in Him, you have no fear. There is literally no fear of the unknown at all. This is because you take on the challenges of life head-on and know that you have the backing of our Lord and Savior, Jesus Christ. This way, no matter what decision you make, you can make it with complete confidence. That's a real positive change, and that will encourage others around you to do the same. Christ's love can change the world around us, and the best part is that we all will be able to sharpen the spiritual dullness in ourselves and our lives. When we speak of spiritual dullness, we need to not only enrich our own lives with the love and grace of our Lord and Savior Jesus Christ but of others too. We, as Christians, are duty-bound to spread His message of

Love and Truth to everyone around us. Being alive is our opportunity to do so, and we have our lives to do that, so we should spend each and every minute of the day thinking, planning, preparing, and eventually executing our duties to spread His message to everyone around us. We need to let them know that they also need to spread the message to others they know. We need to do this because we need to save the rest of mankind from sin. There are so many others out there dealing with spiritual dullness like we have been. We need to do them service just like we are doing to us as well. This will only increase the pleasure of our Lord and Savior, Jesus Christ. We can help build God's Kingdom here on Earth, and our Heavenly Father will be so pleased because we are not just making an effort to fix ourselves but others around us, too, and encouraging them to help fix others around them too.

The simple rule of thumb, after all we have discussed so far, is that opportunity simply waits for no one. God will provide you opportunities to strengthen the connection you have with Him, so we always have to be prepared. This way, we will cash in on that opportunity and get even more close to Him. The idea here is to plan and prepare before moving into new areas. Those areas are the ones you identify are tainted by spiritual dullness and need to be sharpened. Once you plan and prepare properly, then miracles will happen. At the end of the day, it's all about believing in yourself and the Almighty that He will always protect you. So, you should plan without fear and execute, knowing that you always have His back. You will be able to brave the storms without any fear of drowning because you will be rescued. See, faith is that powerful, and in these times that we live in today, we all need something to believe in. There is no one better than our Lord and Savior, Jesus Christ, because He knows what is best for us and will guide us to victory. We need to have complete trust and faith in Him. It is only then we can achieve success in life. It's imperative upon us to have complete faith and trust in him to find success in every aspect and facet of life. After all, He has blessed us with eternal salvation, so we should always be thankful to Him. The best part is that He loves us all unconditionally, and he wants nothing from us other than just faith in Him and that we walk His path. Even if we don't, He will still love us. It is upon us to realize that we are born on this planet for a special purpose. We have faith in Him for a special purpose. We are born to spread His message of love, grace, and truth to everyone around us. Our Lord and Savior Jesus Christ sacrificed Himself on the cross so we can be saved from sin. It's the least we could do, and it's not a lot. We just need to walk His path and honor and love Him back the same way He does to us. I can't stress enough times how much we need to trust Him and walk His path. Whatever happens to us, good or bad, is a test from Him. We need to look at this way. We will only be rewarded ten-fold when we pass those tests. The best thing is that we don't need a cheat sheet to pass it. He will guide us to pass those tests and cross the obstacles and hurdles blocking our path to success in life and the hereafter. We shouldn't take it for granted that we are blessed with eternal salvation. This is why spiritual dullness occurs in our lives because we sometimes could take it for granted that we're Christians and are blessed with eternal salvation. We still need to walk the path of our Lord and Savior, Jesus Christ, and that's how we can truly be called Christians. We need to be prepared at all times because our faith will continuously be tested, and that's where we know how much spiritual dullness we have in our lives. You see, my faith was tested in the same way. When I lost my job, it was a test of my spirituality. What did I think of before anything else? I started worrying about survival, what I would tell my spouse, how I will take care of my family, and other things. I forgot that this was just a test from our Lord and Savior, Jesus Christ. Perhaps there were areas that were suffering from spiritual dullness, and those needed to be sharpened. I forgot that, as a Christian, I can look towards Him for guidance, and my life will be back on track soon enough. I started thinking that my life is only limited to this world and forgot there is a life beyond this as well. I forgot that our Lord and Savior, Jesus Christ is there to help us through our hardships. I started thinking that it was the end of the world. I wasn't prepared to face these tests because I was happy with the way my life was going. I had a job and was able to take care of my family's needs and my own needs. Things were fine because I had no worries at all. I was living a stress-free life until my life turned upside down and made me reassess my life. I got panicked at the time, and I totally forgot about the reality of life. Unfortunately, our material world and the rat race for material wealth make us lose touch with our own reality. We forget the truth and start living in a fool's paradise. We keep fooling ourselves, thinking there is no tomorrow. We think that our life is just limited to our current existence, so we should live our lives to amass as much wealth and money that we can. We forget that there is a force out there that is more powerful than we can ever imagine, and it is that force that controls everything in our lives and our world. Nothing moves without His power. He is none other than our Lord and Savior, Jesus Christ. It is He who has control and power over anything and everything in the world and our lives.

He can change our lives with a snap of His fingers. This is something we have to realize. Every problem we face is a chance for us to reassess our lives and our circumstances. It is an opportunity to set things right, and once that is done, set those in motion. Then, we can get out of the current hurdle or obstacle blocking us from the progress with His guidance. Speaking for myself, I got the same realization after losing my job. I thought I had lost everything, and there was no way out. The truth is that there is always a way out. We just need to look out of our material lives and existence to see that we are not alone. In troubled times and happy times, in fact, in all times, our Lord and Savior Jesus Christ is with us. We need to simply look towards Him for guidance, and then we can find a way out of our own troubles. If we had always been walking His path, if I had personally been walking His path, then I would not have thought the way I did. I wouldn't have panicked or worried so much as I did when I lost my job. Once I realized and remembered that there is a force greater than all of us, that's when I changed my thinking and decided to walk

His path. That was the day my life changed, and believe me when I tell you this, I never looked back. I knew that if I need to change my life, I need to change myself first, and then my circumstances will change too. Change truly starts from within. That's when I could change things around me, and those around me will be impacted by my positive change. That's the time when we look beyond our own material existence. We have a much greater purpose in our lives other than amassing wealth. While money is a necessity, it's not the purpose of our lives at all. See, I wasn't prepared, so I suffered. I now know that there will be more times ahead that will test me and will be even tougher than what my predicament was at the time. I wasn't prepared for the test I faced, so I had then learned my lesson. I then prepared myself for all future tests to come, no matter what form they take. No matter what obstacles and hurdles would be placed in front of me, I was no longer afraid. I knew that by walking the path of our Lord and Savior Jesus Christ, every test will be made easy for me. As stated before, faith can definitely move mountains. It can change lives too. It can make the impossible possible. As Whitney Houston and Mariah Carey once sang in "The Prince of Egypt" soundtrack, "There can be miracles when you believe," miracles can happen when you have faith. We need to keep this in mind at all times so we cannot just succeed in life in whatever we're doing and also please our Lord and Savior Jesus Christ. Any problem or issue we face in our lives is a chance to reassess our spirituality, so we shouldn't take it negatively. It is an opportunity to fix our spirituality and our relationship with our Lord and Savior, Jesus Christ. If we weren't prepared, we have a chance now. This is very important for us to realize that we can change ourselves. It most certainly starts from within, and then that change can impact others to look within themselves and change for the better. Michael Jackson once sang, "I'm starting with the man in the mirror. I'm asking him to change his ways." This is true because we always need to ask ourselves and check ourselves to see how prepared we are for whatever catches us by surprise. It is imperative that we always keep this in mind. If we are prepared, we can plan our lives accordingly and even perform better. Our entire outlook needs to be changed, and it's not hard at all. What we're required to do is no rocket science. Faith is perhaps the easiest thing to attain because we gain so much by having faith. At the same time, it should be unselfish and sincere. Our Lord and Savior, Jesus Christ, knows what's in our hearts. We can lie to others and even to ourselves but not to Him. He knows us better than we know ourselves. Sincerity and honesty go a long way, and the more sincere and honest we are with us, others, and to our Lord and Savior Jesus Christ, we can be better prepared to face all hurdles in life. We can take on all problems, tests, and hurdles head-on without fear at all. Fear is never an option because when we have faith in Him, no force on Earth can stop us from getting to where we want to be in life. This is something we should never forget and keep applying it in our lives. Success will come our way. In fact, success will chase us instead of us chasing it.

In the end, I want to re-emphasize one thing in particular. When we talk about planning, preparing, and performing, we need to think like a military general. If you're a good chess player, then you know that preparation is very important in the game of Chess as much as it is in military warfare. A good book to emulate military strategies in real life is Sun Tzu's "The Art of War." This is one book that can be a great guide to dealing with life's issues by thinking as a military general. Knowing your enemy, planning the attack, knowing the weaknesses and strengths, and then executing the attack is all part of military strategy; that's how we need to live our lives too. We need to think like a military general at all times. Now, here's one more thing I must add to make my point clearer. See, every military general plans and prepares, but he also has a wealth of advisors, captains, and lieutenants at his disposal. Mostly military advisors act as consultants to the general and help with the overall strategy and planning. It's very much like a tea effort, and that's how many strategies are set. Here's another example to illustrate my point. If you are a fan of association football or soccer or any other major team sport, then you will see how much planning and preparation goes into each game. Each head coach is tasked with leading his club or country's side to glory in different competitions. Let's make things easier and say you're a head coach of a soccer club in Europe. You have a hectic season, which involves rotating your squad through different matches in different competitions and tournaments. Your job is to train the squad, build your youth setup, plan and prepare for each match, strengthen the squad via player transfers, and getting rid of unwanted players. At the same time, you need to manage the club budgets and finances and make sure you're not overspending on anything. You also have to keep the board, fans, and players happy at all times. There is a lot of pressure in the job, and sackings happen every now and then. A few wrong moves these days and a bad patch can lead to a sacking. A highly influential player gets upset, and the fans retaliate against the head coach. Sacking is almost inevitable in these circumstances. Most recently, Lionel Messi of FC Barcelona wanted to leave the club because of a bad result against another top European club, the German champions Bayern Munich and the manager was sacked around the same time. A new manager comes in and changes things from top to bottom and releasing highly-regarded players and club stars. Messi gets even more upset, and the head coach or manager gets the pressure. Ronald Koeman is the new manager at FC Barcelona, replacing the outgoing Quique Setien. That's just one example of what happens in the soccer world. If you fail to live up to fans and board's expectations, then you're bound to be sacked. It could be ensuring survival in the top division or winning it or the top European club competition such as the UEFA Champions League. A lot of objectives are there, and they vary between clubs. Even with all this crazy planning and preparing, the head coach isn't alone. He has a host of coaches at his disposal and assistants to advise him. There is an Assistant Manager at all times to help out or even take over when the head coach isn't available. As a head coach, you have an entire team working for you to ensure results, but the key decision-maker is you. When we translate this into our real lives, we also have a host of advisors, consultants, and coaches. These days, life coaches have become as effective as therapists. See, in our lives, we have the same team at our disposal. When we are born, most of us are lucky to have parents and siblings alive long enough to give us advice on everything in life. Now, none of these advisors and consultants can advise us better than the greatest planner in the universe and beyond. That's God. Our Heavenly Father is the greatest planner, and He doesn't need a team because He is very self-sufficient. He doesn't face any pressure or has any obligations. We need to please Him rather than the other way round. When we need to plan and prepare in life, should we not trust the greatest planner in our lives? This is the point I am trying to get at in this chapter. We can plan and prepare all we want, but the greatest planner is God. In every transition, turning point, and challenging times, it is the best planner who will guide us, and if we trust

Him, he will make us prepared for what's to come. We don't need a whole team when we have God. That's how powerful God is, and without Him, we are absolutely nothing. We can prepare and plan all we want, but nothing could have prevented the COVID-19 pandemic from happening. Nothing could have prepared us for that. However, if we stayed true to God and held on to His rope much better, then we would have planned, prepared, and performed a lot better than we have. In our life, preparation and planning is key, but a lot of times, we get these curve balls thrown our way. We can't be prepared for unforeseen circumstances. We can't be prepared for a loved one's death, especially if it's untimely. Sometimes, we just can't plan and prepare for these, and they do very likely throw us off guard. This is very important to understand that if we always hold on to the rope of our Lord and Savior Jesus Christ, we can be prepared for anything. COVID-19 changed our lives, and we lost our friends and loved ones. It was no act of terrorism or war. It was just a deadly pandemic we were never prepared to face as a world. This is why none of our humanly advisors can help us prepare better than the greatest planner. If we continue to hold onto His rope, then we will always be prepared and will plan effectively. Them, we will perform and execute and be successful in whatever we do, and if we work together through this, then we can defeat the COVID-19 pandemic once and for all by taking the guidance of our Lord!

5

Delayed, Determined, & Destined

"You speak of destiny as if it was fixed." — Philip Pullman, the Golden Compass

"But as one was cutting down a tree, the iron ax head fell into the water." — II Kings 6:5a

In this chapter, we will be referencing the same passage from II Kings 6:5: But as one was cutting down a tree, the iron ax head fell into the water. The idea here is if you lose your edge, you'll slow your progress. Since the iron ax head fell into the water, the son of the prophets was unable to cut more trees. Hence, it slowed his progress. He would require another ax or at least another iron ax head to fit on the ax to resume cutting. What does that mean for us in our spiritual and practical life? What does it mean that we lost our edge? Now, if I bring up my life example of losing my job again, this was the time I basically lost the edge- for all practical reasons. I had lost the means to earn a living and support my family. I had lost the means to enjoy life the ways I was used to, including a few luxuries I would desire every now or then. Even more so, I had lost my self-confidence and self-esteem because I was no longer employed. I felt down and depressed. I was afraid to confront my wife because I didn't have the guts to open up about my predicament. I wished the drive back home could simply be an endless one, so I don't have to go home and deliver the bad news. At that point, like the woodcutter in II Kings 6:5, I had simply lost all hope. I had no way to go on. I didn't realize at the time it wasn't the end of the world. It wasn't the end of anything at all, but it was just a new beginning. Sometimes we don't know it, but we do need a new start. Situations happen in life, which forces us to change our direction in certain ways. It goes back to the same mantra: adapt, endure, and persevere. By losing all hope, I simply lost the edge.

Basically, I had come to the point that I had lost everything I had gained so far. That is very much far from the truth. There will be other jobs and employment opportunities. I would just need to beef up my resume so I can apply for better or similar positions. I would need to sharpen my skillset by learning some new skills in the time off and apply for better positions too. The opportunities were all out there. I just had to swim in the ocean and fish the right one out. By swimming in the ocean and unable to float, I will simply drown. Hence, I should not swim in that ocean and drown but stay above water and seek out those opportunities. The opportunities are there, but all we need to do is look for them. If we work hard enough, we will find them. We will find them a lot easier if we continue to look towards our Lord and Savior Jesus Christ for guidance, and that guidance is the greatest gift He bestows upon us. We need to share and spread this gift with the rest of the world so that anyone in our predicaments could take guidance and inspiration from the Carpenter of the Universe.

The point I am stressing here is that by losing the edge, we slow progress. It's okay if things don't go our way at times. We can simply give up hope or take the challenge head-on. Slowing down progress is only doing us more harm than good. I could utilize the time off work productively and secure interviews and work on getting another job. It's not rocket science. It's simple. Life throws us hurdles, and God tests us with those hurdles. We can either give up hope or slip into depression. What happens next is that slowly the connection with God gets weaker and weaker. We then have to work even harder to restore that connection. The reason is that we slowed our own progress. We need to recognize that God always has the best interests for us. This is the same message we're carrying forward in this chapter. The point is when it comes to loving God and walking in His path, we can't afford to slack off. We can't make excuses because God knows us inside out. He knows us better than we know ourselves, so we can't get away with any excuses at all. The choices are in front of us. What do we do? Shall we get upset that the ax head is drowned in the water? Or shall we make a new ax? The opportunities are endless. We just need to look for them and find them. As discussed in the previous chapter, we should not hesitate to seize that opportunity. We need to make ourselves prepared to seize upon the opportunities God sends us our way to get closer to Him. These times of transitions and transformations are the testing ones. If we realize we have lost the edge and slowed our own progress, all we need to do is lift ourselves up and work on re-establishing that connection. It's never too late, but the later you are, the more progress you'll be required to make. Having said that, I must stress that it's absolutely never too late to make a difference in your life. I can give you my own example. The realization hit me when I first lost my job and kept contemplating my next move and my family's reaction on the long drive home. That time was my time to make a difference in my life. That was the opportunity. Sometimes we get so lost in the moments that we forget that there are better opportunities out there for us, but all we need to is to look for them and seize them. That's where the magic comes in. At first, we need to check and see if there is a distortion in the connection between ourselves and our Lord and Savior Jesus Christ. Once those checks are performed, we need to re-establish and reconnect with Him and then look for those opportunities. With true faith, the opportunity will be knocking at our doorsteps, and we will realize that we are a better person, a better Christian, and in a much better place in life thanks to that opportunity.

We can apply this to spiritual dullness too. The more we are slow in handling the tests God puts us in or lives, the more we are slow to regain that connection that bound us to Him. In every facet of our lives, we need to examine where our spiritual dullness lies and how we sharpen the dullness that is entirely up to us. We could simply lose the edge and spend our entire lives sharpening our spiritual dullness. That's something we should never want ourselves to be in because that will throw us in a downward spiral. In order to get back up, it will simply take way too long. Once we identify areas of spiritual dullness, we should develop a plan to sharpen those areas in our life, and we should simply seize on that opportunity and act on it. As the prophet stated, "Write the vision and make it plain upon the tables that he may run that reads it Habakkuk 2:2. Once the progress starts, it will take less time to restore our connection with God. Basically, we need to realize it, and I can't stress it enough that time is of the essence. Time waits for no one. Time once gone, can never return. We can't turn back the clock. This is why we should never hesitate. The idea is simple: prepare, seize, and act on the opportunity that presents itself. Things will work out the sooner you re-establish the connection with God. The more you delay, the more your progress and eventual success will be delayed. This is why it's essential to always stay tuned to your inner voice and be connected to our Lord and Savior, Jesus Christ. This way, you will be able to maintain your progress and attain success in life and beyond at the right time. Time never waits for no one, but the truth is that it's never too late to turn to the Carpenter of the Universe for guidance.

This is because He loves us more than anyone else in the world and cares for us. He wants us to live better lives and only asks us to keep faith in Him.

Another saying that fits here well is from the book The Golden Compass. It is spoken by Philip Pullman and goes like this, "You speak of destiny as if it was fixed." Is our destiny fixed? Can it be changed? Do we control our destiny? These are interesting questions that we will dive into as we move along in this chapter.

The way our lives are, despite our most utmost planning, things don't always go as planned. We should always make room for contingencies. This way, there's always a backup plan. What I am trying to get at here that nothing is fixed. While our lives may be in the hand of God, there is still room for free will. There may be different paths to our ultimate destination, and we chose those paths. Things then fall into place, where plans pan out, and sometimes, they don't. However, God's guidance through his grace makes the journey both bearable and exciting. David suggested that God is constantly guiding our footsteps, “The steps of a good man are ordered by the Lord: and he delights in his way” Psalms 37:23

The fact of the matter is we already know we are destined for everlasting life. That comes with faith in Jesus Christ because he sacrificed His life for our sins. That lets us know that as long as we keep believing in Christ, then our future is secure. We just need to look towards Him at every point in our life, good or bad. That’s how we can find the edge. By doing so, we will keep uncovering areas of spiritual dullness and sharpen them by re-strengthening our relationship with Christ. That’s our ultimate goal. No matter how many logs fall in the water, we will find a way out because Christ, our Lord, is with us always and forever. As long as our faith is strong with him, we will always find a way out of our troubles. This is true because no problem or issue is too big or too small for God. As long as our faith remains strong, our problems become His problems. In a matter of time, we will see our faith in Christ being redeemed.

If He can sacrifice himself for our sins, then imagine what he can do for us in our times of need. This is the ultimate sacrifice, and it keeps on giving and giving as long as we keep our faith strong. We should consider ourselves lucky that we are Christians and are destined for everlasting life. We just need to live a life as God intended for us to live, and everything else will easily fall in place. That's the beauty of faith. It simply keeps on giving without any diminishing returns at all. In Job 8:7, it is said, "Your beginnings will seem humble, so prosperous will your future be." While you may struggle during a challenging phase in your life, your outcome will be prosperous. This is because you are holding on to the rope of your Lord and Savior, Jesus Christ. Patience and perseverance are two traits that are absolutely necessary traits to have in the pursuit of a prosperous outcome. We need to follow the examples of the prophets because they are our role models. They have persevered and remained patient while suffering, and they went through all their respective challenges to prove a point. You can overcome the odds and conquer your challenges as long as you have faith in the Lord Almighty. You can read the Old Testament and find examples of the sacrifices made by Abraham, Moses, Noah, Job, Jacob, Joseph, Lot, and so many others who withstood suffering but ultimately became the victor thanks to their relentless faith in our Lord and Savior Jesus Christ. Their stories are examples for us to follow. Our challenges can't even compare to the ones they have faced, so we need to steadfast in faith towards our Lord and Savior Jesus Christ. In 40:31, it is said, "but those who hope in the LORD will renew their strength. They will soar on wings like eagles; they will run and not grow weary, they will walk and not be faint." This is the kind of spirit we need to have. The ultimate faith in our Lord and Savior Jesus Christ will allow us to face any challenge with full courage. We will become men and women of steel because we believe in the Carpenter of the Universe. We should shower praises to our Lord for His grace. It is He who gives us hope. In Peter 1:3, it is said, "Praise be to the God and Father of our Lord Jesus Christ! In his great mercy, he has given us new birth into a living hope through the resurrection of Jesus Christ from the dead," It is this belief that our Lord and Savior Jesus Christ was resurrected and is our Messiah, is what makes us Christians and that is key to eternal life. We are absolved from all sin as we were born sinners, but faith in Christ has made us sinless. Hence, we need to walk His path at all times. Problems will happen, and life may come to a standstill, but we should never give up hope. No matter what has happened in the past, we should remain steadfast and strong in faith towards our Lord and Savior Jesus Christ. In Isaiah 43:18-19, it is said, "Forget the former things; do not dwell on the past. See, I am doing a new thing! Now it springs up; do you not perceive it? I am making a way in the wilderness and streams in the wasteland." The past can't be undone, but our future can still be fixed no matter how late we think we are. That's the attitude we must have, even when things don't go as planned. In Jeremiah 29:11, we are reminded that: For I know the plans I have for you," declares the LORD, "plans to prosper you and not to harm you, plans to give you hope and a future. Our

Lord and Savior have plans for us, even if we think that things aren't going our way. That's where patience and perseverance come in, and it goes a long way, as I have seen for myself in my life.

Now, we have seen that when things don't go plan, and there are flaws in execution, things slow down. There are obstacles and hurdles in our path to our destination or ultimate goal. We may lose hope or completely give up because, at that time, we don't know what to do. We don't know how to cross the obstacles or hurdles because the path is laden with thorns. Time isn't slowed down, but progress ultimately is. There are a few ways that we can tackle our issues going forward. The easy way out is to give up. However, that isn't recommended at all and not even as a last resort. The reason here is that we end up losing all the progress we have made so far. All the hard work will be in vain. For example, I did lose my job. However, I had years of experience that I had accumulated on my resume. Progress had slowed, but that didn't mean I should give up. By giving up, all these years of experience would go down in vain. All my hard work would mean nothing if I gave up. Lack of progress or slow progress was my time for reflection. It was time for me to reflect back on life about how it has progressed so far and what changes need to be made to get my life back on track. It was perhaps an unplanned vacation from corporate life. Perhaps it was time for me to spend with my family because corporate life had kept me too busy and away from the people that mattered. I was making money but losing time with my family. It's all about looking at the glass half full or half empty. Either way, you look at it, it's the same thing. There two sides to every coin. You can give up in life or buckle up and get back on the saddle once you are prepared. The slowdown in progress gave me time to plan my next steps, as I mentioned above as well. It gave me time to carve out a new game plan in life. Perhaps it was time for me to go for a job that evens out the work-life balance so I could give my family the time they deserve from me and that I was unable to provide for them because I was too busy working. It may not be a higher salary, but at least it would allow me to spend quality time with my family, which we realize later on in life is so important. The rat race can really wear you down. Once you're settled in life with a spouse and children, you realize that the rat race hardly matters. You just want to work to provide for your family and the rest of the time you want to give to them. You want to save enough to take them on vacation. At the end of the day, perhaps that's what God wanted me to think about. While it's merely an example, this is something that applies to everyone. We need to simply keep faith in God's plan because He knows us better than we know ourselves. He simply knows what is best for us and what isn't. We don't need to worry about fixed destinies, predetermination, and fate because not everything is in our control. We only need to know that we are just destined for everlasting life. That life is not of worries or troubles or planning. There won't be any contingency plans. We are simply working and living to eventually get to that destiny, no matter what road we take. The only thing that matters is faith in God.

The idea that we are simply discussing so far is that the way things play out in our life is simply a bit too complicated for us to understand. That's simply the way our lives have been from the beginning. We don't choose where we are born, to whom we are born, and what we look like. We don't choose our names. We don't choose a lot of things about ourselves when we are born. We don't even know what faith we are born into. We eventually discover all these things as we grow up. We realize who the important people in our life are. Interestingly we don't even know who our siblings will be. When we are born, and as we grow older, we don't even know who our spouse will be. Life is simply a voyage of discovery, and that's why things are so exciting for us as we grow from simply an infant to an adult. What's even more interesting is that we don't even know when we will die. When there are so many things we don't know about our lives, then there is really no need to worry so much. It all boils down on our relationship with our Creator.

Since our own life is in the hand of God, then why is there a need to worry about anything in the future? If a storm is coming, we should be braving it. If we don't know who we will even end up marrying or where we will eventually end up going to university or what career we'll have, then we should treat life as an adventure in faith. Things may not work out as planned; while we have goals and milestones we want to achieve, the probability of achieving almost anything is 50/50 on average. We can work towards our goals, and the probability gets higher. In the movie "The Pursuit of Happyness," Chris Gardner, as acted by Will Smith, was quoted to have said, "Don't ever let someone tell you, you can't do something. Not even me. You got a dream, you got to protect it. People can't do something themselves, they want to tell you, you can't do it. You want something, go get it. Period..." The simple fact here is that if we have enough faith in Jesus Christ, our Lord, and Savior, then anything is possible. Even when there are delays in plans and goals, that's all part of Christ's plan. We learn to be patient, and this allows us to tackle the different problems that we face in life from birth to death.

Patience here is key. Whatever we set our sights on is achievable. Just look at the achievements mankind has made in aerospace, communications, engineering, and technology. We have discovered and landed on the moon and other planets such as Mars. We have broken the communications barrier making long-distance communication a thing of the past. It’s like the person is right in your neighborhood despite sitting and talking to you from the other side of the world. We have progressed from horses to cars, airplanes, and space shuttles. All these signs of progress have taken years and years, and it's not like there were hurdles. These hurdles were overcome, and progress was made. Change is the only constant in life. We need to understand this very well that our faith gives us a lot of power. We have the gift of everlasting life. We can pursue anything and achieve anything as long as we are willing to go the distance. This is the ultimate power that we derive from our faith. It is due to Jesus Christ that mankind has come so far in the 21st century. We could never imagine the life we were living today five decades ago. We are living in a time where there are self-driving cars! Tesla automobiles are pioneers in this field. Could you ever imagine a car driving by itself even twenty years ago? We used to see these television shows like Knight Rider and the Batman movies. All this incredible technology is created by mankind, which itself is a creation of our Lord and Savior Jesus Christ. This itself is an incredible testament to the power that we have been gifted from our Lord. A century from now on, we can't even imagine how far mankind will go. Some of us reading this may not even live that long to see the transformation the world will take at the time. The bottom line here is that we don't need to worry or feel bad when we face problems and hurdles in life. For Jesus Christ, no problem is too big or too small. We will lose several logs in our life, but at the end of the day, our continued faith in Christ will guide us and take us to our destination. It's the most incredible feeling. I must tell you that we have all of this within ourselves, and once we feel the power of our faith, we can simply move mountains. It's the privilege that comes with believing in Christ, and I can't tell you how fortunate I feel. So, whenever you feel that you have lost a log in life, simply look towards Jesus Christ, our Lord, and Savior, and you will find the way.

The idea in this chapter is to convey the message that all that is good and bad in our life is simply part of God's plan for us so we can learn to adapt, overcome and persevere. Many of us face several personal and professional hardships in life, and they take a huge toll on us emotionally and sometimes physically. I've mentioned my job loss and unemployment phase quite a few times, and this is something a lot of us can relate to. Then, there are problems that are so common in life, such as the death of a loved one, divorce, separation, trauma, parental issues, emotional, physical, and sexual abuse, and even fear of the unknown and paranoia. We suffer each and every time when we face such experiences. I've only scratched the surface of what we humans have to endure in life, which can send us on a downward spiral that we can never ever recover from. It is the sad reality of life. Some of us can take these experiences so negatively that we can become extremely negative ourselves. We can face fear, insecurities, and even suicidal thoughts- which is the worst negative feeling that we can experience. Just imagine that we are gifted with everlasting life thanks to our faith in Jesus Christ, our Lord, and Savior. When we have been promised eternal life, suicidal thoughts should never cross our minds, no matter how worse the situation we have found ourselves in. Some of us have made such horrible mistakes and committed crimes and found ourselves in dire straits. Some of us have found ourselves locked behind bars. We are serving time in prison. These are the harsh realities of life, but thankfully for all of us, there is one ultimate reality of realities. There is one reality we can find support in and peace with. This one reality is our Lord and Savior Jesus Christ, which is above all of these painful experiences. We need to raise ourselves up so high towards Him that all these painful experiences will feel very small. If we keep telling ourselves we can't adapt, overcome, and persevere, then we never will. We can hurt ourselves more than others, unfortunately. No matter what the situation is, the presence of our Lord and Savior Jesus Christ is always shining down on us from up above. You see, His presence is everywhere. We just need to embrace his presence, and we shall overcome. We shall persevere. We will eventually succeed in our goals. We will pull through. We will find peace because peace lies in our faith in Jesus Christ. This is what moves us forward as believers in Christ, as Christians. We should never forget the gift that we have been given, and that gift is very powerful. No matter how worse the situation is, we will find a path, and we will be guided thanks to our faith in Christ. Fear, paranoia, insecurities, and even suicidal thoughts will never cross our minds. Our faith in Christ will allow us to overcome it all. We will keep renewing ourselves as we keep renewing our faith. It is a fact that we have to adapt to changes in life and the times we live in. Similarly, at every such point in life, our faith will be tested time and again. This is why we need to renew and strengthen the relationship with our Lord and Savior Jesus Christ at every turning point in our life. We need to feel the power so that all of these life problems will easily be solved.

6

Shape, Sharpen & Shine

"We become what we behold. We shape our tools, and thereafter our tools shape us." — Marshall McLuhan

"Iron sharpens iron, so a man sharpens the countenance of his friend." — Proverbs 27:17

Human beings are social animals, and we were born in this world to form communities and spread the message of our Lord and Savior, Jesus Christ. We have come into the world, making friends, relationships, and some of us have found true love in others. While it is my firm belief that true love only comes in the form of Jesus Christ, if someone else embodies that same true love, that's the one person we would like to have a relationship that could be friendship or something greater.

The idea here is that it takes another person of equal strength, gifting, and talents to shape us. There are so many others in Christ who share the same values as us, and we can learn from them. They can mold us, and we can mold them. The fellowship is an important part of Christianity. It builds communities, and together we can do Christ's work here on Earth.

Interestingly, the Marshall McLuhan quote, "We become what we behold. We shape our tools, and thereafter our tools shape us," most likely talks about man's relationship with the tools they make. It is something we have seen for years as to how the industrial revolution at first, and then later, the communications revolution has shaped our lives. Our tools, our machines, our gadgets have shaped our lives. We prefer commuting in cars, texting on our phones, and staying in touch with friends on social media. Our technologies have shaped our generations. It's an incredible relationship between man and machine. We've become more reliant on technology more than ever before. It would be strange to remember that perhaps two or three decades ago, we lived without such modern communications advancements that we have seen today. Ironically, we did survive that time well. Despite the lack of advancements compared to today, we were fine. We were happy with the way things were, and I am sure that two or three decades from now, we will look back and remember this time the same way.

In Christianity, we let our fellow brothers and sisters shape and mold us, and in turn, we do the same for them. The role model for all of us is none other than our Lord and Savior Jesus Christ. We inspire each other and help each other become better Christians and walk the path of Christ. We help each other uncover spiritual dullness in areas of our own lives and personalities and sharpen those areas. At the end of the day, we are all one in Christ. So we are all destined for everlasting life. In this way, we are all of the equal strength, gifts, and talents as followers of our Lord and Savior, Jesus Christ. As we immerse ourselves in fellowship by doing different things such as Bible study, or community service, or anything that gets us closer to Christ, we help our fellow brothers and sisters in Christ walking that path much better. We can look towards our Church community leaders, pastors, and ministers for guidance. It's a learning process, and whether we are just a believer or a pastor, we can learn from each other. Knowledge is power, and the more knowledge we share with each other, we grow as Christians. We grow as believers in Christ who want to walk in His path and emulate Him at every step.

While the ultimate gift we all share is everlasting life, which comes from the belief in our Lord and Savior Jesus Christ, each of us is endowed with spiritual gifts and talents. According to the website of the Seventh-day Adventist Church North American Division, "According to the Scriptures, these gifts include such ministries as faith, healing, prophecy, proclamation, teaching, administration, reconciliation, compassion, and self-sacrificing service and charity for the help and encouragement of people."

Each one of us is endowed by one or more of these spiritual gifts, and we need to find those among us that are equally gifted and talented so we can grow upwards in faith. We can pass on the gifts to others so each of us can harness our collective talent and gifts together. All of these heavenly gifts are part of us, and they come from our Lord and Savior Jesus Christ, who was endowed with all of them. In order to walk His path, we need to make full use of them.

The Proverbs 27:17 quote says, "Iron sharpens iron, so a man sharpens the countenance of his friend." We use this reference to emphasize on the same fact that two of us who are equally gifted and talented spiritually can help each other uncover those spiritually dull areas of our lives. Iron sharpens iron, and in the same way, we can sharpen one other among ourselves too. It's about helping each other stay connected to our Lord and Savior Jesus Christ and strengthen our relationship with Him at every point of our life. We have a natural tendency to be social, and we can't live our lives on our own. We have parents, spouses, children, friends, and other relatives that we turn to in times of need. We also have our brothers and sisters who we do fellowship within Church. We are defined by our family and our community. This harkens back to the Marshall McLuhan quote about the relationship between man and his tools. Men designed tools or rather machines that enriched our lives and became an extension of our lives. This happened so much so that these simply became a part of our lives that we have become completely dependent upon. Having said that, we need to find the same kind of equally gifted and spiritually talented people in our communities so we can elevate each other. We become an extension of each other's lives the same way man and machine became for each other.

We need to seek out meaningful relationships in life that help us grow in Christ. We can find those relationships in our spouses too. We can be equal partners in a marriage, and if our spouse is as equally talented and gifted in spirituality as we are, then it's a win-win for everyone. Since we spend our entire lives with our spouses, these could be the best spiritually gifted partners one can have. It's the beauty of such a marriage that binds us together to our spouse for all eternity, and as it's often heard: till death do us part. We both can share the gift of everlasting life from our Lord and Savior Jesus Christ together. We can lift each other up because of the equal spirituality we share and our love for our Lord and Savior Jesus Christ. Our spouses can help uncover spiritual dullness in every area of our lives and personalities, and this will help us grow as Christians. It's important to realize that the right spouse can change your life for the better. The spouse you choose to marry and spend your entire life with can easily make or break your life. We need our spouses to enrich our lives, and in turn, we have to enrich theirs. There is a reason why it's called 'holy matrimony!' When we get married as Christians, we get married in the name of our Lord and Savior Jesus Christ. It's not just a union of two people. It's a spiritual union too. Our partner will grow old with us and will be with us through all times, thick and thin. It is not just up to our spouse to uncover spiritual dullness within us. It's also our responsibility to uncover the same in them. It goes both ways. This way, we both can collectively hold on to the rope of our Lord and Savior Jesus Christ and continuously re-strengthen our relationship with Him.

These rules don't need to necessarily apply to life partners and marriage. Throughout our lives, we need to find individuals on an equal level to us spiritually so we can lift each other up. Those could be family members, Church friends, work colleagues, or even mentors. Although I feel mentors may be on a higher plane than us when considering spiritual gifts and talents, but they could at least match our level when needed. The idea here is to seek out these individuals all our lives. If we are in college, we should try to seek out those people in our classes and even religious societies on campus grounded in Christian ministry. We can definitely find like-minded people, and once we get to know them better, we could tell if we are on the same spiritual plane as them. Christian fellowship societies in college are popular places to find such people. You could end up with a roommate who isn't Christian and show him the Word of Christ, and if they convert and join your path in walking the path of our Lord and Savior Jesus Christ, then you may have just found your match, that person is now at the same spiritual family as you and you can lift each other up. While all these feel like hard tasks, we need to remind ourselves that our Lord and Savior Jesus Christ didn't have it easy at all. In fact, we all know he sacrificed Himself to atone us for sins so we can be saved. If he gave the ultimate sacrifice, then why can't we make sacrifices of our own in life too when needed. Walking the path of our Lord and Savior, Jesus Christ, maybe hard sometimes, but we know He is with us at all times. When we know that is the case, then we don't need to worry. Our life is a journey of self-discovery, and when we find our spiritually talented matches, we can make them part of our lives in many ways. As stated above, these don't need to be just life partners at all. All throughout our lives, we end up meeting in different settings, and even when we travel the world, we can find the same. Imagine one of us living right here in the United States finds an equally gifted and spiritually talented person on the other side of the world. How awesome would that be? Travelling definitely helps, and the more we travel, the higher the chances of meeting such people become. The idea is to always keep searching for those people.

In my life, on a daily basis, I aim to meet people who are equally spiritually gifted and talented as I am so we can lift each other up. There are days I don't find anyone, but when Jesus wills it, I will find that person. I look for those in my family, my circle of friends, and my Church. Often times, I would seek the help of my wife too, who has worked very hard to get me the kind of connections I am looking for. At the same time, I always ask my friends to introduce me to their friends who they feel is an equally spiritual match to me. It's so much fun, to be honest, and I end up making a lot of friends, and we then make our Bible study groups where we learn and understand the divinely inspired word of Jesus Christ together. The feeling I get from such sessions is incredible—the kind of conversations we have to help us grow so much in Christ together. We would always find ourselves planning spiritual retreats where we could solely focus on the life of our Lord and Savior Jesus Christ and lift each other up to an equally higher plane. These are things you all must try, and believe me, you will find your spiritual matches. If you are single, then it is highly recommended to find that spiritual match in your spouse to be. You'll realize how much it will benefit you as you start your lives together. If you truly have faith in our Heavenly Father, then you will find that person that can complement your spiritual gifting.

There are Godly people everywhere, and I want to reiterate in the end that it's very possible to find them. I want to summarize here that we need to keep our faith so strong in God that He will automatically connect us to the most important people in our lives. We will have the best of friends and life partners. We will lead prosperous lives because all these connections are those that came from God. All of these people who entered our lives and made a difference ultimately came through to us because they also were looking for spiritual partners and guides like we were. These are the people we need to bond with. If we work together towards holding on the rope of God, then we can all be blessed at all times. Prosperity will come our way because God's light will shine through and guide us at all times. This is how we meet the right people and form an entire circle of friends and family who are connected to God the same way we are. We're all part of God's one big family, and to show our allegiance towards Him, we need to always hold on to His rope. He is going to bring us success, happiness, and prosperity at all times.

7

Limits, Losses, & Locations

"So the man of God said, where did it fall? And he showed him the place." — II Kings 6:6a

In life, we go through many changes and meet several challenges. It's not always easy to take on challenges. Sometimes a challenge comes our way, and we lose the edge. We've talked about this in the previous chapters, but there's one thing we always forget to identify when we come across hurdles in life and face challenges. That one thing is quite simple, but sometimes we do indeed forget or overlook it. We have talked about why we lose the edge previously, but we haven't discussed where we have lost the edge. We need to know where we have lost the edge, and that's also important than asking simply why and how we lost it. In order to gain help, we must need to determine where we lost the edge.

To understand the phenomenon of where we lose our edge, we turn to the passage from II Kings 6:6a, "So the man of God said, where did it fall? And he showed him the place." Here Elisha is asking one of the sons of the prophets where the iron ax-head fell. The son of the prophet shows him the place where he lost it. This is the same principle we must apply in our daily lives, too, because we also need to know the place where we lost our edge and use that to gain help in recovering the edge. To understand it even further, I will return to my example of the time I lost my job. I was sitting in my car driving home and wondering what I will tell my wife and how she will react when she finds out about me losing my job. The fear turned into paranoia, and I became afraid. I thought this is the end, and there is no hope in sight at all. Now that I know where all the negativity started and that's where I started losing my edge. That's the time I know I should seek help. It's only a job loss, right? My life isn't over; I am still alive and kicking. I can still get back to my feet if I look for other opportunities. I needed to go back to the point where I lost my job, and that's where I lost the edge. That's the same case with all of us, but we Christians are blessed with a gift that others who don't believe aren't. We all know what that gift is. It's the gift of everlasting life. See, things always fall back into place. We can lose the iron ax-handle many times in our lives, but all we need to do is figure out where we lost it. That's where we will find the edge, and we will find it because of the gift of everlasting life.

You need to realize that every turning point in your life, Jesus Christ is with you. He is one we look upon at all times. In times of need, happiness, and tragedy, He will always guide us through. He is our Lord and Savior. He made the ultimate sacrifice by sacrificing himself on the cross. He washed away all our sins so we can get everlasting life. Every time it feels like we have lost the edge, we need to retrace our steps back to where we first lost it. That's the key. We all know nothing in life is always easy. However, by holding on to the rope of our Lord and Savior Jesus Christ, we do find a way out of troubled times. Let's walk through some real-life scenarios that any of us could experience at certain times in our life. For example, we are facing a troubled marriage, and divorce is on the cards. We have tried to straighten things out with our spouse, involved family, and friends, and done everything to fix the marriage, but we're simply running out of time and options. It's a terrible time for you and your spouse. Let's put a further spin on this. Let's say the marriage is only five years old, and the five years have been great, but trouble has been brewing behind the scenes, and it has just reached a fever pitch. Problems have surfaced and have become very difficult to resolve. It seems like a dead-end no matter what you try to fix problems with. You've even tried couples counseling. You've tried everything, and you just don't know what to do. The ax hand has fallen so deep you don't know what to do. When one is in such a situation, you must be thinking while reading this, what can anyone do? How could you rescue the marriage? Does it have a chance?

Is going separate ways the only option? Is taking a break from each other a better option? Does it have to end in a divorce? Is there no easy way out? See, we don't honestly know which outcome or option is the best or worse for us? That knowledge only belongs to our Lord and Savior, Jesus Christ. So you may ask what can be done. You may kneel down in prayer and asking the Lord for help, but you still feel hopeless. There is a way out, and you aren't doing anything wrong. Holding on to the rope of our Lord and Savior, Jesus Christ, does help. You may have to be patient, but it does help. However, there's one thing that really needs to be done, and that's where holding on to His rope really counts. If you want to know the answer, it's quite simple, really. You simply have to retrace the steps where you lost the ax the first time, albeit a proverbial one. In the case that I just mentioned, all you would need to do is retrace the steps all the way back to the time when you can pinpoint the very first time problems that occurred between you and your spouse. You need to go back in time and remember what exactly started all the mess in the first place. When you do that, you'll realize what actions resulted in the problems and the ultimate chaos that has invaded your married life. You need to go back to the root of the problem and then solve it from there. That's where holding on to the rope of our Lord and Savior Jesus Christ will really help because through His guidance, you will find a solution to the entire mess and be able to find peace. You will have to then wholeheartedly accept the resolution because eternal salvation lies in believing in our Lord and Savior Jesus Christ.

Now I will return to the earlier life example of my job loss. Here's how I will retrospectively solve the matter by applying the same principle I applied in the example above. I will go even further deeper into the crux of the matter to explain my point here. I've already explained I need to go back to the point I lost my job and where I was at that time- driving a long commute home. You may be wondering how deep I need to go back to figure out how to resolve the issue at hand. If I want to go even further deeper than that point, I need to go way back when I first realized there were issues that surfaced at the workplace that affected my performance and eventually led me to my dismissal from my job. Once I went back to the absolute begging where the issues first occurred, I can figure out what I did wrong and how I could avoid these issues if they ever resurface again on my next job. As human beings and even Christians, we are bound to make mistakes, but we should always learn from them. As Christians, we know that we were born sinners, but by believing in our Lord and Savior Jesus Christ, our sins are simply washed away, and we are destined for eternal salvation. No matter how big or small the problem is that we are facing, by simply going back to the root of the problem, a solution can be found. A marriage could potentially be saved if we go back to the root cause of the problem. We try to figure out where the first marriage problems occurred, and then we see how things built up from that point. Once we determine the root cause of the problem, we could find the solution and work from there. Perhaps, we may just be able to save our marriage if our Lord and Savior Jesus Christ wills it. I've illustrated the two examples in this chapter that can apply to all of us at any time in our life. I would not wish any of your problems, but I am just trying to explain how to handle problems when they get very serious. The rule of thumb is to simply determine the root cause, see what caused what, and how things went from bad to worse. Once you determine the history of the problem, then a solution can be found, and that is something we can apply to any issues and hardships we face as and when they happen. Sometimes things may get out of hand, and that's okay. We don't always have control of things and how they play out, but we can at least find ways to resolve them, and the one way we have examined in this chapter is quite useful definitely.

By giving an example of my job loss and a hypothetical marriage issue that can happen to any couple, I have explained how we end up losing the plot on where things go wrong. The idea here is to always go back to the root cause, the absolute beginning where the issues started. You will realize how helpful this exercise proves to be. At the same time, you must understand that if you truly believe in our Lord and Savior Jesus Christ, He will show us a path out of the trouble we are in, and that could be anything in life. The way our lives have become now, problems are part and parcel of daily life. We need to consult and talk to Him every day so he can keep showing us the light. Just remember, a lot of things that happen to us are a series of causes and effects. Every action is a reaction and a reaction to an action. By going back to the initial cause or action, we can deduce where things started from and apply corrective actions. Sometimes it may be too late, but we can always learn from those times. Life is a series of experiences, good and bad, and everything that happens to us gets us closer to our Lord and Savior Jesus Christ. This is the reason I have stressed time and again throughout the book to look towards Him at every turn of our life. He will always guide us!

8

Miracles, Mantles & Mandates

"But out of limitations comes creativity" — Debbie Allen

"So, he cut off a stick and threw it in there." — II Kings 6:6a

We have all heard the saying, "necessity is the mother of innovation." This holds very true, especially as far as the human race goes. The way humans have progressed in the fields of science, technology, and innovation is incredible. The world has changed a lot in the last two or three decades. A lot of the advancements that have taken place have come out of necessity, especially in communication. That is always an area that will continue to improve as the years go by. As mankind advances, what about each of us as individuals. How do we personally advance and improve ourselves. We have heard the saying that out of every crisis comes an opportunity. It's quite simple, and both the above sayings are focusing on the same things, which include change, innovation, and opportunity. Let's throw in one more quote for good measure. Debbie Allen is quoted to have said, "But out of limitations comes creativity." See where I am going with this? The idea here is that we are constantly evolving and changing. It allows us to tackle issues and solve crises. Now, the question I want to touch upon is what if the problems and crises are related to our faith. What if all this becomes a question of faith? Then, what do we do? How do we go about solving these problems? In the previous chapter, I discussed how we should go back to the root cause of any issue that we are facing in life to find solutions and, at the same time, hold steadfast to the rope of our Lord and Savior Jesus Christ. In this chapter, we will look at how we can turn a crisis into an opportunity and use our limitations to the best and creative ways possible with the guidance of our Lord and Savior Jesus Christ.

The most beautiful thing about our faith is that we already have the answers. All we need to do is look at them in our Scriptures. The Old and New Testament both offer so much guidance that we can easily live our lives without looking towards anywhere else. Our books possess so much knowledge, and that knowledge can be a positive guiding force for us all our lives. Much of the Scriptural references I have provided are from the passages in II Kings 6. One such line from the same passage that fits so well here is the following: So he cut off a stick and threw it in there. This is from II Kings 6:6a. The idea here is quite simple. So one of the sons of the prophets cuts off a stick and throws it in the water. This is the miracle that God helps him recover the sharpness that was lost by using the very element that caused the dullness to help as a means of recovery. Our Lord and Savior Jesus Christ uses objects that expose our dullness to help in recovering our spiritual sharpness. The point here is quite simple. Human beings aren't perfect. We are fallible beings, and we were born sinners, but only through belief and faith in our Lord and Savior Jesus Christ, we are gifted with eternal salvation. Salvation comes through Christ and Christ alone. Our limitations don't pose to us as hurdles, but we can use them to create opportunities and innovate. We are blessed with creativity, so we use that to our advantage, just like the son of the prophets did. He cut off a stick and threw it in the water. He didn't give up but used his limitations creatively to create opportunities. This is the same way we need to recover from spiritual dullness. The stick was an object, and similarly, we need to find those objects too. Sometimes, all we need to do is look inside ourselves and, with the guidance of our Lord and Savior, Jesus Christ, discover those objects to rediscover our spiritual edge.

I'd like to go back to my personal life example here again. What's really interesting here is how that incident in my life taught me so many different ways to recover from spiritual dullness. Spiritual dullness is a normal thing, and there are creative ways to recover from them. We have touched upon several different ways to do just that in the previous chapters. Now, whenever we have an issue like the job loss I keep coming back to, we need to look for objects through our Lord and Savior Jesus Christ's guidance and use them. Now, what options can one person think of if he loses his job? He would start applying for openings in other companies in the hopes of landing a job. What if the process is taking time? You need to have some revenue coming in to support yourself and even a family if you have one. It's very interesting to see that humans are naturally entrepreneurial. Find what you're passionate about and keep praying to our Lord and Savior, Jesus Christ, for guidance. Once you have discovered your passion, look for like-minded people, and work on starting your own business. There are always freelance options available too. The object here we speak of is not a tangible object but something that lies deep within us. It's our passions, and those drive us forward. The idea here is to be creative. Think of ways to build a recurring income while you're looking for better opportunities. If the freelance work gets big and you land more clients, then you can keep doing that. Similarly, if the business you start with like-minded people gets established and starts growing, you can simply focus on that. A job loss is a crisis situation, but you can see how I showed that it can become an opportunity to be creative and stand up on your own two feet without working for someone else. Social media and the internet has made it easy to start your own business and create income streams. The opportunities out there are endless. What's interesting here is how we can use technology to find solutions for ourselves. That itself can be an object. The internet is a wonderful resource, and you can find your big break if you look hard enough. At the same time, we need to absolutely positively do one crucial thing. We always have to hold on to the rope of our Lord and Savior, Jesus Christ. It is through Him, we can use these objects, tangible or otherwise, to find a way out. We can find our spiritual edge. There is so much you can do if you just hold on to that rope.

No matter how big or small any problem is, there's always a solution. We shouldn't let these problems and crises open doors for more spiritual dullness to enter our lives. It is better to tackle them head-on. History has proven time and time again how much progress mankind has made. This goes back to what I touched upon earlier when speaking of progress. Humans are the most talented of all God's creations. From earlier times, we discovered how to create fire from wood, and then the Industrial Revolution happened. We saw how humans moved from horses and camels to cars, airplanes, and even spaceships. We started off with ships and sailed all over the world. Then we flew all over the world and eventually into space. We have discovered more of our beautiful universe. All of this progress has happened in the 20th and 21st centuries. While human beings are talented, but we are also limited, as stated earlier. Despite our limitations, we have come so far as a human race; there was never a time we let our limitations get the better of us. The communications revolution has changed the world so much today. We started off with telephones if you remember the rotary kind! We would send letters via post, and today, we do it via email, instant messaging, and social media. Then so many years later, after the invention of telephones, came cellular phones. These days, we can't live without our cellular phones. What's so fascinating is that even cellular phones have evolved into smartphones.

Everything today is at our fingertips. Just thinking about all the progress mankind has made so far makes me forget about the problems I face in my life. It's the incredible power and knowledge that we have gotten from our Lord and Savior Jesus Christ, we have come so far. If you study very closely at the progress of mankind from the early days to the 21st century, we have found one thing in common. Do you see how every progress has been created via the use of objects? From cars to airplanes to computers, objects are involved. Whether it's a silicon chip or wires or the engine of an automobile, these are all tangible objects. We see such amazing creativity considering the limitations of us being human beings. It's honestly the thirst for knowledge that has brought us so far. The most amazing thing that I see is that human beings haven't stopped thirsting for knowledge at all. Knowledge is power, and it can help solve so many problems. We've touched upon just science and technological innovations up till now. I am even more amazed by the innovations made in medical science. While there are still many diseases that are incurable today, cures to several diseases have already been found. On a daily basis, our scientists all over the world are constantly searching for knowledge and ways to find cures to incurable diseases or find better cures to curable diseases. So what would we define as the object to be here? The object here at its core is not tangible but very much intangible. I would define it simply as knowledge, Human beings have pushed themselves to find cures, and that's why the field of healthcare has grown so much. If you are reading this and asking yourself who is ultimately responsible for all this progress in the fields of healthcare and medical science, it is definitely none other than our Lord and Savior Jesus Christ.

Throughout all of the ages to the Communications revolution, He has been with us all along and will continue to be. This is all the more reason we need to continuously hold on to the rope of our Lord and Savior Jesus Christ and look towards Him for guidance.

Just think about it for a second. If, through His blessings and the knowledge he has bestowed on us human beings, we have made so much progress, can't we just look up to Him to figure out solutions to our problems. We should never look at our limitations as obstacles at all. We should look at these limitations as simply opportunities. We should never give up because, in our minds and hearts, we should feel and absolutely believe that there are no limits whatsoever to what we can do if we continue our search for knowledge and be creative with the opportunities that crises present to us. Life is absolutely no bed of roses, but it's also not entirely a bed of thorns either. Even though we aren't perfect, but there is so much perfection bestowed upon us from our Lord and Savior, Jesus Christ. It's a really wonderful feeling when you think about it. No problem is too big or small for Him, and honestly, just believe in Him as our Lord and Savior is all we need for eternal salvation. There is an intangible object here as well and that I would define as simply faith. It has been said that faith can move mountains, and most certainly, it can if you choose to not only believe but constantly and continuously hold on to the rope of our Lord and Savior Jesus Christ. What I am trying to say here is that if you believe in Him so strongly and are always with Him, there is so much you can achieve in life. We can be masterminds of our own individual revolutions. We can make incredible changes in our life that can benefit generations upon generations. We can set a precedence that our future generations can follow. We just need to find that object, intangible, or tangible, to figure out a solution to whatever issue we face in life. When your belief is strong in our Lord and Savior Jesus Christ, it is when you can be the most creative. It is then our faith can definitely move mountains. It is when we can achieve what we once thought was impossible. It all about believing in Christ and then believing in your own abilities and gifts that He has given to you to accomplish milestones and solve problems.

I will reference the movie "The Pursuit of Happyness" here again. Based on the life of Chris Gardner, Will Smith plays the title character to perfection. It is more than just your regular rags to riches story; it's more about believing in yourself and achieving your goals. While it's not a Christian movie, it does show the many ways our Lord and Savior Jesus Christ works in improving our lives. It shows Christ as a man who, like many of us who have lost our iron ax handle many times in life and now want to find a way out of our life's problems. We see the same concept played out in Chris's real life and the movie based on it too. He uses an intangible object to get through life's hurdles. Here's a man who has pretty much lost everything except his sanity. He has no home to go to, and he is just moving all over San Francisco with his young son and is trying to make a life for himself. His wife has left him, and he just has his son to take care of. He's shown in the movie taking refuge in the bathroom of a BART station with his child. He pulls himself up from there and eventually finds a successful career as a stockbroker. What does he use to pull himself up? What intangible or tangible object does he utilize to sharpen that dull edge in his life? The answer is quite simple. The object is intangible, and it's actually is his will power. He doesn't let anything stand in his way. He survives until he finally attains his goal. Will power, as you can see here, is extremely powerful. If you want something bad enough, you will get it. This is the message the movie repeats at regular intervals throughout its running time. It just shows that the human spirit itself can't be broken completely. What I am trying to explain here is that this undying will power I speak of comes from our faith in our Lord and Savior Jesus Christ. It is through our faith in Him, we can achieve anything. Nothing really is impossible. You need to believe in yourself and your own abilities and put faith in our Lord and Savior, Jesus Christ. The path will be open for you. In the 1999 blockbuster science-fiction movie The Matrix, the character of Morpheus, played by Laurence Fishburne, tells the protagonist Neo, played by Keanu Reeves, "I'm trying to free your mind, Neo. But I can only show you the door. You're the one that has to walk through it." Similarly, in our own lives, our Lord and Savior Jesus Christ opens many doors for us throughout our lives. We just need to watch out for those doors and just walk through them. He always opens paths for us, and all we need to is to simply hold on to His rope for all eternity. The objects that we use to sharpen that spiritual dullness could be many intangible things. It doesn't only need to be our will power, but our dedication to a cause and our determination, among many things. The guidance comes from our Lord and Savior Jesus Christ as it is He who helps us use these intangible objects to get to our destination. In my opinion, if there is one intangible object you should use throughout your life to get out of hurdles should be your undying belief in our Lord and Savior Jesus Christ. That itself constitutes an object because it is the belief in the being that created us. The truth lies with our Lord and Savior Jesus Christ, so why not take the help of His unlimited and infinite guidance to get to our goals and achieve our dreams. The answers to our troubles lie within us, and we need Him to find those answers. Look to him, and you will find what you seek!

9

Resurface, Re-emerge, & Reappear

"Beneath your burdensome regrets and who you think you are through the lens of past mistakes, there is someone beautiful who wants to emerge."— Bryant McGill, Simple Reminders: Inspiration for Living Your Best Life

"And he made the iron float" – II Kings 6:6b

Over the course of the chapters, we have looked at many different ways we uncover spiritual dullness in different areas of our lives and within us. We looked at ways to sharpen those areas so we can restore our connection with our Lord and Savior Jesus Christ. In the previous chapter, I discussed how we can use objects, mostly intangible, to find ways out of troubles in life. The one thing I emphasized is how we can use our faith in Christ to reach our life objectives and goals. In this chapter, we will see how we use our faith in our Lord and Savior, Jesus Christ, to renew ourselves. Basically, we will look into how a new person can re-emerge from within us. We can be born again.

In II Kings 6:6b, it is written, "And he made the iron float." You see one very important aspect of our faith here. Our Lord and Savior Jesus Christ can literally do anything. He can change our lives with the snap of His fingers, metaphorically speaking. In very simple terms, He can make anything and everything happen. We see that in the passage quoted above from II Kings, the ax head resurfaced underneath the depths of the water buried deep. This is something we can apply to our own lives. The water can be a personification for our heart. It has been said that our Lord and Savior Jesus Christ lives in our hearts, and we need to look deep inside our hearts to find the answers to our problems. This is because that is where guidance lies. In all the chapters, I have emphasized on many occasions that we need to look upon Christ for answers to our problems and continue to hold on to His rope. Many of the problems we face within our lives are buried deep within our hearts. It only through God's power to resurface issue that we are sometimes afraid to face can we truly discover the power of God's anointing and presence to deliver us from our fears. Even though when issues that are buried in hearts are being resurfaced by God's power, we must make the decision to face these problems head-on with God's grace to gain personal victory.

There's one quote that fits very well in this chapter. Bryant McGill was quoted to have said in the book 'Simple Reminders: Inspiration for Living Your Best Life,' "Beneath your burdensome regrets and who you think you are through the lens of past mistakes, there is someone beautiful who wants to emerge." See, we all make mistakes in life. None of us are perfect. We have made mistakes in life and will continue to commit mistakes as long as we are alive. Mistakes are normal, but there is one thing we need to do when we make mistakes. We need to learn from them. This is how we and grow into better and mature human beings and Christians too. One other thing I would like to reinforce here is that we are born sinners. Due to this reason, we will continue to sin knowingly and unknowingly. However, there will come a time in our life when we will take a deep, long, and hard look at ourselves and where our life is heading. That is when we realize that we are missing one key component that will make us eternally free from sin. It is when we realize that there is a being and a higher power much greater than anything we can ever imagine. He is none other than our Lord and Savior Jesus Christ, and it is He who guides lost souls that have spent their lives swimming in a deep pool of sin. We can gain lifetime redemption from our sins by doing just one thing. We need to reestablish our connection with our Lord and Savior, Jesus Christ. Where will we find Him? He is everywhere, but most importantly, as I stated above, He lives deep in our hearts and souls. It is there we need to look for Him and find him and restore our faith with Him; we become born again that way. In other words, we receive a kind of spiritual awakening. We basically become what pop culture would call "born-again Christians." While this has become a very common term, the media uses to define those people who have sinned and have rediscovered Christ. What we will see in ourselves is something very different. We will see a radical change within us. We will become better human beings and will stay away from sin. We will work harder to improve our lives and also better the lives of others around us. We will walk the path of our Lord and Savior, Jesus Christ.

To be reborn isn't a bad thing at all. Don't let pop culture make you think you're trying to wrap wool of purity around yourself. The truth is that we all need to examine our lives and see where we're going wrong. We all need to go through turning points and transitions in order to become better human beings. As Christians, we have a responsibility to our Lord and Savior, Jesus Christ. We look to Him for guidance, and if He allows us to be reborn with a new motivation in life and a new direction, there is no harm in that. Never be embarrassed to express your faith and love for God because He made us who we are, and He is always there for us. This entire book is about finding yourself and reaching inside yourself to become a new person. There is no harm in shedding aside your past to be a completely new person. Our past is what we can learn from, but our present and future are what we can still control. The decisions we make today will have an impact tomorrow. That's why we, as God-fearing Christians, we need to examine our lives at all times. In previous chapters, I had mentioned the example of the pop star Madonna. I will mention her again as she is one of those popular recording artists and performers who has constantly been reinventing herself to appeal to the times. As you know, musical trends have changed every so often, so almost every other album of hers sounds different from the other. It's still Madonna's voice, but it's a new sound or a different style or theme to the album. Now, Madonna is not afraid to change according to the times. She has changed her music and her own personal style to suit the times. Many times, she has been a trendsetter, especially in her early years in the 1980s pop music explosion; young girls everywhere wanted to be like Madonna and copy her looks, haircut, and style. Madonna was cool, and being like her made one feel cool. Having said that, if Madonna isn't afraid to change or reinvent herself for commercial gain or to appeal to changing musical trends and a growing and diverse fan base, what's stopping us from changing ourselves to please our Creator. The point I am making here is if we're mocked for being 'born-again Christians,' then its okay. We should be proudly wearing our faith on our sleeves. At the end of the day, we're doing all this for the love of God. There's no greater love than that. We don't need to be a pop star, but we just need to be our true selves. We need to be honest with God and ourselves. To be guided by God is a blessing in itself. We should never take this for granted because God touches everyone, but only when we truly understand His Love and Grace, only then can we allow ourselves to change. As always, change comes from within us but guided by our Lord and Savior, Jesus Christ. That's something we need to understand, and it's very important as we keep looking for transitions and turning points in our lives. Sometimes, they happen as we roll with the punches. See, no one is greater than God, but we can become great because of His Love and Grace. It's very powerful, and we can only realize the power once we experience it ourselves. I have experienced this, and that's why I have written this book to encourage others to try it themselves. Each and every one of us goes through some tough times, and I started my book with a personal example. I had spoken about my job loss and how that impacted me so much. It was only when I reached out to our Lord and Savior Jesus Christ for guidance, it is only when I brought the change in myself from within. I looked towards Him for guidance, and I survived. The idea here is that each and every one of us can do the same, and that indeed shows the power of faith. As stated before, faith can move mountains, and when faith is that strong, it can move people too. When it moves you, it can move others. You can use your faith to inspire others to find the change in their lives that they have been seeking for so long. There are so many real-life examples of people who have changed, and while I have spoken for myself, you can look up the internet and find such inspirational stories that will most definitely move you. Some of them will shake you to the core.

One example I can mention here is the professional wrestling business. That business has been riddled with controversies for decades. Professional wrestlers or sports entertainers have known to undertake a very hedonistic and drugged-fuel rockstar lifestyle thanks to their bigger paychecks. At the same time, they have taken so many steroids to keep their body in perfect shape; they have ruined themselves. So many professional wrestlers have gone on the dark side and totally lost it. One example is Chris Benoit, and the less said about him, the better. However, there are several positive examples, such as Steve Borden and Michael Shane Hickenbottom. Steve Borden found fame in the squared circle as Sting. He has several personas, and the surfer and Crow persona were his most famous ones. What some wrestling fans may or may not know about him is that he is a famous born-again Christian. Sting is a positive role model as he has continued to play his iconic character on television for decades, although he is retired now. For many years, he has also preached his faith and openly talked about how he got saved by our Lord and Savior Jesus Christ. Now, you may be wondering who Michael Shane Hickenbottom is; if you haven't searched him on Google, you'd be surprised to know he is none other than one of the most popular and cherished pro wrestling superstars and entertainers of all time. He has been given so many plaudits such as "Mr. WrestleMania," "The Showstopper," and "The Main Event." The man is speaking of the Heartbreak Kid Shawn Michaels. Shawn Michaels was an evergreen presence on television since the mid-1980s and became a huge superstar in the 1990s when he became the world champion in 1996 when he beat Bret "Hitman: Hart at WrestleMania 12. Despite being famous as initially part of the Rockers with Marty Jannetty, and later as a solo competitor, he had to deal with a lot of his personal demons. Those included indulging in drugs and a hedonistic lifestyle. He had become the world's biggest superstar working for the WWE (then WWF) but had lost his way. Fame and success followed him, but he was a lost soul. Many of his peers have said that he has been difficult to work with and was a huge influence on WWE owner Vince McMahon. Shawn Michaels had gone on the dark side during his break from wrestling between 1998 and 2002, and during that time, many of his friends in the business, such as Kevin Nash and Paul "Triple H," Leveque tried to help him but to no avail. However, help came in the form of his wife, who was once a WCW Nitro Girl named Rebecca. She encouraged him to turn to our Lord and Savior, Jesus Christ, and be saved. He got saved, and then things changed. He became a better wrestler, and his career reached newer heights. He had seen a transition and turning point in life where he turned to God, and he became a completely new person. He was still the Heartbreak Kid but a much better version! If HBK can do it, so can we. He is also proud to talk about his Christian faith and how he changed his life, thanks to God's Love and Grace.

While the above concept talks about renewing our faith with our Lord and Savior Jesus Christ to become a new person, this same concept can apply to many other facets of our lives. We have a life that is full of so many obstacles and hurdles as we live and grow. Over the course of our lives, we will encounter so many problems and hurdles. So many times, we're stuck in tough situations; it is in those times we realize we are in the state of spiritual dullness. This is something that has been discussed over the course of the previous chapters. We have covered many ways on how to find solutions to our problems via our own faith and relationship with our Lord and Savior Jesus Christ. In this chapter, we will focus more deeply on how to renew and reemerge as better humans and better Christians at the same time through our faith. This is also one way to solve problems and overcome obstacles. Each one of us has the power and abilities within us to solve problems. We have discussed how we can use our limitations creatively and find ways out of life's obstacles in a previous chapter. The idea then was the same. Those creative energies lie within us. We need to look very deep inside our own hearts and find that courage to overcome any obstacle that comes our way. All that is part and parcel of the process of renewing our relationship with our Lord and Savior Jesus Christ. The one thing we need to realize and accept is that change is the only constant in life. We are always changing and evolving as we grow and mature. We all have dreams and aspirations. Those dreams and aspirations mold us as we grow. They define our lives for us and, at the same time, the purpose of our lives. We dedicate our lives to the attainment of those goals and objectives, and we live our lives accordingly. We choose our spouse, friends, and our careers accordingly to fit those goals and objectives. Over the years, we will trip, fall, and stumble. This will happen not once, but on many occasions. At no point, we need to think that we can't do it. We can't achieve our dreams just because we made a few mistakes. At that point, if we do end up giving up, we will lose everything, and I mean everything that we have gained so far. We have heard the saying that life is short, so we should live it large. The idea is to live a fulfilling life. There are two aspects to that fulfilling life. The first is personal fulfillment, and then the most important, above everything, is spiritual fulfillment. Both of these go hand in hand. At every point in life, when we fall and stumble, all we need to look deep inside our hearts and find our Lord and Savior Jesus Christ. Once we re-establish that connection with Him, we can be back on the path to both spiritual and personal fulfillment. That is when we will find ourselves again. We will rediscover ourselves and find it within us to overcome any obstacle in our path and achieve what we once thought was impossible. We will be on the path to our own personal and spiritual victory. You see, by reestablishing our faith with our Lord and Savior Jesus Christ, we have already been reassured that we have earned the gift of eternal salvation. The rest of our personal victories, goals, and milestones will continue to follow.

The point here I am trying to make is that life isn't a bed of roses. In fact, it's a bed with roses that have thorns and those that don't. You just need to avoid picking up the roses with thorns or be so strong that the thorns don't pinch you. Another thing to note here is the idea of reinventing yourself. This entire chapter is about reemerging and renewing yourself, being born again, and so on. One thing we tend to forget is reinvention is so common in our world today and has been for so many decades. Reinvention takes place in everything around us, and that includes our fashion, taste, styles, pop culture, music, and even technology. As we all know, change is the only constant in life, so changing for the better is very normal too. Apple releases a new iPhone every year and markets it with all the hype stating it has some amazing, awesome, and cutting-edge features that no other phone has. Each year, they are reinventing the iPhone, making it better so they can have consumers invest in it. In order to do it successfully each year, they are constantly improving the iPhone. Similarly, why can't we reinvent ourselves or even improve ourselves each year to please our Lord and Savior Jesus Christ? I think that's such an amazing way to sharpen those spiritually dull areas in our lives. All this requires is a deep evaluation of our own lives and see how we can become a new person. Don't forget one important thing. We do have divine guidance, so don't be afraid to change or accept change, because change is a consistent part of life, and it will always happen. The change will always be positive if it's through the assistance and guidance from our Lord and Savior Jesus Christ. All this requires is placing complete trust and faith in Him and just let yourself go and be open to change. You will be a much better version of yourself, and that's the transformation that needs to be quite regular. There's always room for improvement, and since we aren't perfect, there will always be room to grow and be better as time goes by.

Reinvention, reemergence, or renewals- all of these points to more or less the same thing. We, as Christians, have to always strive to be better in walking the path of our Lord and Savior Jesus Christ. All we need to do is look inside our hearts and see where we need to improve. Change comes from within, and if you hold on to the rope of our Lord and Savior Jesus Christ, it will be very positive. You will feel like a new you every time you do this. You'll shed away your old self and become a completely new person. Think of it as a spiritual reawakening, and it's such a beautiful feeling. To be honest, it's hard to describe it for me, but I know this much. You only know its true essence once you experience it yourself. I can tell you this much that I have felt it, and it was ecstatic. I would never recommend any advice unless I've tried and tested it for myself. I don't mind being called born again because, to me, the only happiness that matters is in walking the path of our Lord and Savior Jesus Christ. What the popular media describes people like me who have renewed their faith in our Lord and Savior Jesus Christ has no effect or impact on me at all.

I've used this example quite a few times in this book, but this life example resonates with me with a lot and something I can relate within so many different ways. I will harken back to my example of the time when I lost my job and the long drive home. Believe me, when I tell you this, the drive was perhaps the longest one for me going home. It may not be physically, but it was most definitely a mental one. I was so deep in thought in that drive because that time, I would say, was the turning point in my life in so many ways. It was truly a life-changing experience for me. See, anyone in my position will feel hopeless and scared about the future. No salary coming anymore, relying on savings, and dealing with the aftershocks and reactions of the family like the wife and children. All that made the time the scariest for me. I knew that I couldn't stay unemployed too long, I would need to alter my lifestyle, and I would have to worry about getting the bills paid in time. Severance pay would only last so long. These were obvious concerns I had, and I did feel like it was the end of the world for me. I thought it was the end of the road, and my life is over. These feelings of despair and hopelessness are pretty normal for many people who lose their livelihood.

However, we quite conveniently forget that there is a being mightier than all of us. He is our provider, and He will never leave us without hope. That being is our Lord and Savior, Jesus Christ. He always has a plan for us. My job loss led me to my spiritual reawakening. When everything goes wrong, we do look at God, but we need to make a promise to Him and ourselves that we will change. We will walk in the path of our Lord and Savior, Jesus Christ. We will need to look deep inside our hearts and find it within us to rise again, to be born again. That's what I did, and I took control of my life again. I was rescued by the love and guidance of our Lord and Savior Jesus Christ. If you ask how that happened, it all had to do with me looking very deep in my heart and connecting with Christ. Once that connection is established, it changes your life, your world, and your worldview completely. You just look at everything life throws at you in a different way. You look at life through the eyes of our Lord and Savior, Jesus Christ, and when you experience that, the feeling is surreal. It just takes over you. All negativity and negative thoughts escape your mind. In due course, you make the right decisions, and things fall back in place. Every time we stumble in life, it's God's reminder that we should look towards Him if we have forgotten Him. Then once we renew our relationship with our Lord and Savior Jesus Christ, we become a new person each time. This spiritual reinvention is very beautiful, and one should embrace it with open arms.

In the movie, The Pursuit of Happyness, Chris Gardner, played by Will Smith, literally lost everything. As stated previously, he lost his home, was separated from his wife, and had to take care of his child and himself while being virtually homeless and jobless. With his marriage at stake and no means of earning a livelihood, did he give up? The movie is based on the real-life story of Chris Gardner, who became a successful stockbroker from humble beginnings. You see, Chris never gave up. He saw in himself and looked deep down in his heart that he had the will power to conquer everything that life threw at him. Ultimately, he became a winner in life and achieved his ambitions. He reemerged a new person, and that's the beauty of human will power. A famous quote by Chris in the movie goes as follows, "Hey. Don't ever let somebody tell you you can't do anything. Not even me. Alright? You've got a dream, you've gotta protect it. People can't do something themselves; they wanna tell you you can't do it. You want something, go get it. Period." See, anything is possible if you believe in yourself and your ideals. We gain strength, as Christians, from our Lord and Savior Jesus Christ, and it is He who makes things happen. We consistently have to look deep down inside ourselves and make sure that the connection is maintained. Every time we reemerge as a "new me," we gain one step closer to our Lord and Savior Jesus Christ, and in turn, our goals and ambitions too.

Man can and has done so much already. See, with the love, guidance, and grace of our Lord and Savior, we can achieve the impossible by looking deep down in our hearts and reinventing ourselves. That's the crux of the message in this chapter, and I would urge all of you readers to give it a shot and experience the spiritual reawakening and reinvention I have also experienced. Reinvention is key to improving yourself and making yourself better at every turn of your life.

10

Confess, Confide, & Conduct

"We must build dikes of courage to hold back the flood of fear" – Martin Luther King

"Therefore, he said, Pick it up for yourself. So he reached out his hand and took it" – II Kings 6:7

The previous chapter spoke about looking inside your heart and finding yourself all over again by reconnecting with our Lord and Savior Jesus Christ, through which we can reemerge and reinvent as new persons. The central idea was to maintain and constantly renew the connection with our Lord and Savior Jesus Christ so we can become better Christians. We find our way of all obstacles and hurdles the same way. In this chapter, we go a bit beyond what we have already studied in the last nine chapters. We will once again revisit the concept and idea of finding and rediscovering yourself, but this time we will use another way to find that lost edge. As discussed in previous chapters, we have consistently touched upon dealing with hurdles and obstacles. We've talked about establishing, reestablishing, and maintaining our connection with our Lord and Savior, Jesus Christ. We've talked about self-belief and walking the path of Christ on several occasions. There are so many ways to achieve all of the above, but then there's something that goes way beyond everything we've touched upon. It pretty much sums up everything I have tried to teach and explain to you in the entire book. You may be wondering what I am trying to hint towards. At the end of the day, we really need to ask ourselves what is fully required to pick up the pieces.

The answer here is quite simple, really. What it all boils down to is the fact that you need to have the courage to pick up what you previously lost and start utilizing your edge again. That is clearly what is required. We can gain inspiration from the Holy Bible too. Quoting II Kings 6:7, "Therefore he said, pick it up for yourself. So he reached out his hand and took it," we need to rediscover the courage within ourselves to pick up the fallen pieces off the ground. No one can change ourselves but us alone. The change will always start within us, but like everyone else around us, we need inspiration. Inspiration delivers motivation, and through that, we find the courage within ourselves to really sharpen that dull edge. It is only then, we can utilize our edge again. Fear is never an option. We should close our eyes to fear. There is only one being that we should fear and fear alone. He is our Lord and Savior Jesus Christ, and it is through faith in him, we can be saved from sin. Fear itself is an obstacle, and it is what holds us back from achieving our dreams and goals. Martin Luther King famously said, and I quote, "We must build dikes of courage to hold back the flood of fear." This is very true. We need to build walls of courage to block out fear from intruding on our minds and senses. These things are of extreme importance for all of us. We can never progress in life if we don't have the courage to strike out fear in our hearts. Bravery is an important trait. Now, if you ask me, what's the best way to stay courageous at all times? The way our lives are these days, we get scared of so many things. Whether it's the fear of the unknown, uncertainty, indecisiveness, or depression, everything leads to fear. If we are courageous enough, nothing or no one can harm us. As Christians, we can easily build those walls of courage ourselves. It's not hard at all because it's all ingrained in our faith. It's quite simple, really. Once we have established and maintained a connection with our Lord and Savior Jesus Christ, we are saved, and we are also bestowed with the gift of eternal salvation. With this gift, we feel unstoppable. Our faith allows us to build those walls of courage and tackle anything and everything our lives throw at us. Whatever obstacle or hardship we face, our faith will guide us and will give us the courage we needed. Such is the grace and love of our Lord and Savior Jesus Christ. We are blessed and extremely lucky to possess this gift of eternal life. Since we have been saved by our Lord and Savior Jesus Christ, why should we fear anything or anyone? Fear should simply be removed from our dictionary and our hearts. We should only fear Christ because he is our Lord and Savior. No one else deserves fear than Him. It is through him we derive courage and the strength to literally achieve everything. Where does that courage lie? As explained in the previous chapter, we really need to look deep inside our hearts to find that courage within us. Believe me, when you find that courage, it's the most powerful feeling that you have ever felt. To have courage is the greatest gift you can give yourself. Being brave and facing all fears firsthand has already won you half your battles. This courage I speak of comes from our Lord and Savior Jesus Christ. The idea here is that you can conquer your fears and live a fulfilling life because you have chosen to walk the path of our Lord and Savior, Jesus Christ. That's a huge step in itself. Then, no matter what happens, you'll always stay strong in the end. As with previous chapters, I will once again return to the example of my life that I spoke of earlier on and repeatedly mentioned it in previous chapters. The day I lost my job has been the day, my life changed. I felt at the time I was at the lowest point in my life. Losing my livelihood and restarting life meant a lot of sacrifices needed to be made. My whole life went into a 360-degree tailspin, and I didn't know what to make of it at the time. I had thought it was bad luck or something on those lines. I had lost everything mentally too. I just had lost the courage to stand up again after taking such a hard fall. I became a broken man and a shell of my former self. I clearly had lost the motivation and drive to go on. It was a huge setback for me at the time. At that point, I had totally given up on life. It was as if I had lost everything within myself to reboot my life. I was consistently concerned about my wife and children. When you reach the lowest of lows in life, you realize there is a point where you can't sink any further. At that time, you'll realize the only way is up. You can rise up out of the water because you can only sink so deep. You can either drown or have the courage within yourself to swim up to the shore again.

You may be wondering what I did to rescue myself from drowning. I had to swim up the shore. Despite facing problems that surface with employment, I had to stick it out and suck it up. I had to do it for my family. I had to do it for myself. Life is full of ups and downs, and this was that time for me. My life had taken a turn for the worst. I was on a downward spiral, and I needed saving. I needed to be rescued. When I had nowhere to turn, a voice called from inside me. This was a sweet and loving voice. It was like I heard my true calling. Something magical was happening at the time.

I felt a transformation taking place inside my heart, body, mind, and soul. It was the moment of truth for me. This was a truth that eluded me my whole life. I looked for it for years, and now it finally dawned on me. I was going through a spiritual metamorphosis, and it was such an amazing feeling. I had realized that I had become way too invested in the affairs of the real world and lost my spiritual edge. I was surrounded by spiritual dullness from all sides. God's voice was calling me, and it was trying to save me from my own darkest depths that I had sunk myself into. It was calling me back to the light. I had closed my eyes to the light for so many years because I had surrounded myself in darkness. It had blurred my vision that I had almost become blind. I had lost all sense of thought, and I just needed a way out. I was called by my inner voice to open my eyes to see the light. The light was dawning on me. I couldn't open my eyes because I had lost the energy within myself to open it.

Thankfully, there was some good news on my way. It was the light and that it was dawning on me so much that it was engulfing the darkness surrounding me. I could slowly feel the darkness around me, turning to light. The light was so bright and powerful that I just couldn't fathom. It was transcending my inner soul. With the light getting so bright, my eyes were being forced to open. I was afraid if they were opened, the bright light would be too much that I would be forced to shut my eyes again. Thankfully and fortunately, the light was warm and comforting, despite it being super bright. My body, spirit, and soul were slowly embracing the light and becoming comfortable in it. Slowly, my eyes would open, and I just couldn't imagine what I saw next. I was starstruck and left breathless. It was the most beautiful light I had ever seen. It kept calling on to me and pushed me to swim up out of the depths of water I had sunk myself in. I slowly and gradually swam up to the shore. When I got to the shore, I felt a radical change within myself. It was like I had become a completely new version of myself. It was like all the guilt, hurt, and sorry over my job loss had all disappeared. I had embraced the light, and the feeling was so powerful. That light had touched every part of my heart, body, and soul. I couldn't imagine the intensity of the feeling. It was unbelievable. I had become a new person inside and out.

You must be wondering what that inner voice was telling me. Moreover, you must be wondering what that inner voice was and where it was coming from. The inner voice was coming from deep within my soul, and it replaced the fear I had with courage. The inner voice was of a being I had blinded myself to. I had blinded myself to His light for so many years. It was finally time to embrace it. It was finally time to save myself and cleanse myself from sin. It was finally time to have faith and receive the gift of everlasting life and salvation. You may be wondering where this gift came from and who was giving it to me. It was none other than our Lord and Savior Jesus Christ. It was He who had woken me up from the deepest depths of my slumber and showed me the light. I had become a new man, this new version of myself was confident and had the courage to take on the world. I had found the courage I needed from the deepest and darkest depths of my soul, thanks to the light that had engulfed me. Our Lord and Savior Jesus Christ had saved me and given me a new lease on life. I stood up tall, proud, and strong with complete confidence and heart to chase my dreams by walking on His path. When you embrace that light, you truly become transformed. My transformation and metamorphosis were complete. I finally had the will and ability to pick up what I lost. If you don't know what that it was, it's quite simple. I had lost courage, and I had rediscovered within the depths of my soul.

We live in a world where pop culture influences us, and we also get influenced by it even more. Motion pictures have a major influence on us, whether its fashion, attitude, or anything else. In the 1980s, pop culture made a huge impact on a lot of our lives. Everything we saw on television and movies became a part of our culture. This continued on to the 90s and beyond. Television shows like Miami Vice became a pop culture icon in their own right. Miami Vice influenced style and fashion a lot, but that's not it. A lot of the shows were about good overcoming evil. It was about finding that lost passion and do the right thing. There is one movie in particular that inspired a lot of young men back in the 1980s. It was the 1986 hit blockbuster movie Top Gun starring Tom Cruise. The movie made him a household name and a global superstar in his own right. The movie portrayed him as a cocky, happy-go-lucky, and confident naval aviator who gets a chance to prove himself and to be the best of the best. In the process, he loses his dear friend due to an accident while dogfighting as part of the Top Gun challenges. He loses not just his friend but his passion and his confidence to be the best of the best. He loses everything that made him so confident in the first place. He eventually rediscovers the passion he lost and finds the courage within himself to move on and graduate with his Top Gun class. He gets called into a crucial mission and becomes a hero. He learns from his mistakes and gets the admiration and appreciation from his peers, especially his now-former rival Iceman. The point is that such movies reinforce the belief that it's never too late to pick up the pieces and find that hidden passion within you. As believers in our Lord and Savior Jesus Christ, it's a lot easier. We just need to put our faith in him, and things will work out. We will automatically rediscover the hidden passion within us that got lost somewhere due to some pitfall in life. We need to find out what matters to us and realize that despite whatever we lost, we can rise up and take charge of our lives. You see, once you've reached the lowest of lows, you can't go any further. The only way you can go is up if you choose to do so, or stay where you are.

Another example from pop culture and the 80s is from the Rocky movies. Sylvester Stallone played the heroic and brave boxer, Rocky Balboa, from Philadelphia who faced challenge after challenge but refused to give up. He fell more times he can count on his fingers, lost loved ones, but was able to pick himself up every time he was down from the same place. He lived to fight another day. One of the quotes spoken by Rocky Balboa from the blockbuster Rocky IV from 1985 was "Going one more round when you don't think you can make all the difference in your life." This is one sentiment that fits what I have been trying to explain in this chapter. There is one very powerful quote from the Rocky Balboa character as well from the 2006 blockbuster hit Rocky Balboa, "Let me tell you something you already know. The world ain't all sunshine and rainbows. It's a very mean and nasty place, and I don't care how tough you are. It will beat you to your knees and keep you there permanently if you let it. You, me, or nobody is gonna hit as hard as life. But it ain't about how hard ya hit. It's about how hard you can get hit and keep moving forward. How much you can take and keep moving forward. That's how winning is done!" That pretty much sums up the crux of this chapter. Giving up is easy, but it's a lot harder to pick yourself up after a fall and live to fight another day.

Life is all about making the right choices. At the end of the day, we are responsible for our own actions and decisions. To make the right decisions, you need guidance and the right guidance. We all know that the right guidance comes from only one entity, and that's our Lord and Savior, Jesus Christ. With the right guidance, we can pick ourselves up from the point where we fell. The point is that life puts us in very tough situations, and we have to constantly pick ourselves up. We are basically the underdogs of our own lives. We are writing our own story, and our goal is to be a champion in our own right. It is about winning and to keep on winning. No matter what it takes, no matter how tough the road ahead is, you need to constantly believe in yourself and work towards your goals. You need to have a firm grip on your Christian faith and walk the path of our Lord and Savior, Jesus Christ, no matter what obstacles or hardships you face. True and eternal salvation lies with Him, and since we are blessed with it through Him, we have a huge responsibility. We have to uphold that responsibility by walking in his path at all times. We have an ultimate goal, and that is to be His champion. A champion never gives up and faces every adversity bravery. He fights with his heart and soul. The making of a true champion is all about guts and glory, and flesh, blood, and tears.

In this entire book, I've tried to explain a lot of things. First of all, this book is about finding yourself and not just yourself – your true self. You need to realize at heart you can only find yourself and your true calling by believing steadfast in our Lord and Savior Jesus Christ. It is He who opens doors for you and helps you get up on your feet when you are down. The way our lives have transformed over the years and decades, life hasn't gotten any easier, so with all the economic troubles and such, we are in dire need of guidance and the right one. There is no better protector and guide of our lives than our Lord and Savior Jesus Christ. He is the Carpenter of the Universe. We talked about various scenarios referencing from contemporary quotes and Scriptural passages, especially II Kings 6, and we studied those to understand the work of our Lord and Savior Jesus Christ in our lives. We need to analyze situations, wait for opportunities, strike when the iron is hot, and leave the rest to our Lord and Savior Jesus Christ. We need to constantly look inside ourselves and remind ourselves each time we fall that this is not the end; this is just the beginning. Every new change in life should be taken positively and not negatively. We should not let the vanities, the sins, and the carnal desires of the world consume us, but be constantly guided by the Carpenter of the Universe, our Lord, and Savior Jesus Christ.

We've learned a lot of valuable lessons through the last 10 chapters. The core message in these chapters is quite simple. You've lost the edge in your spiritual life. You feel isolated and alone and perhaps unfulfilled spiritually. You need to regain that edge by sharpening your spirituality. Spiritual sharpness is key to regaining that edge. It's a lot to do with rediscovering yourself and re-strengthening your relationship with our Lord and Savior, Jesus Christ. It's also about holding on to His rope at all times and walking in His path. Every time you feel like you have lost the edge, you need to reconnect with our Lord and Savior Jesus Christ. All the times, we end up in situations we can't seem to get out of or hurdles and obstacles we need to overcome, that is when we need to look upon our Lord and Savior Jesus Christ the most. The idea here is that as long as you are connected to Him, you will be guided to make the right decisions and overcome any hurdle that comes your way.

The times we are living in are quite challenging. In 2020, we have seen the rise of the pandemic known as the coronavirus, aka COVID-19. This virus has put the world on a standstill. Governments all over the world are panicking, and the citizens are distressed. There is a lockdown in many countries of the world, and everyone is scared about the future. This one virus has taken us hostage. However, this is a time to not be afraid. As stated in the book a few times that with every crisis, there is an opportunity, and we have an opportunity presented before us. We all, as Christians and citizens of this world and human beings, can rally together to save our planet from the coronavirus. This is a time to sharpen those edges that have become dull in our spiritual life. This is the time to regain that connection with our Lord and Savior Jesus Christ and join hands together in faith. We will see and ultimately realize that while our faith and patience is being tested, we will become stronger together and eventually overcome the virus. It may be the catalyst for peace in the world. The problem we are facing is none other than the example of the axe head falling into the water that we have referenced several times in the book. This is our chance to reconnect with our Lord and Savior Jesus Christ and together save our planet from this pandemic that has put the world to a halt. There is no better time than now to make a difference by joining hands together in Christ because He will come to our aid when he sees how much we love Him. He will rescue us because our faith will not be shaken or broken by this pandemic. We will survive and win as long as we keep the faith and apply the principles we have talked about in the book. This isn't the end, it's just the beginning!

Epilogue

"Going in one more round when you don't think you can, that's what makes all the difference in your life." — Sylvester Stallone (as Rocky Balboa from Rocky IV)

"But the one who endures to the end will be saved." — 20 Matthew 24:13

The first quote is the line of dialog from the hit 1985 blockbuster Rocky IV hits right at home here. This is what Sylvester Stallone as Rocky Balboa tells his son before his big international fight with the Soviet champion Ivan Drago in Moscow. He would be training in the extreme and harsh winter of Siberia before he goes tow to tow with his nemesis Drago to win for his country and avenge the death of his best friend and mentor Apollo Creed- who was also once his greatest opponent. Rocky trains in extreme weather with the assistance of Apollo's trainer Duke and later his beloved wife, Adrian. He finds the courage within himself despite facing superior opposition and takes on Drago and wins the match as well as the hearts of the Soviets. This line from Rocky is very important because it's about going that distance when you have lost the courage and will to move on. It's about finding that energy, willpower, and courage to achieve your goals after a failure or series of them. It's about never giving up. Ultimately, that courage and will power comes from God as long as your connection with him is strong as ever and completely unbreakable. That, my friends, is the crux of this final chapter.

After going through 10 chapters talking about regaining that lost spiritual edge, we come to the point where we have regained it. We've come to the point where we have to take that edge and go out swinging. We have to tell life to "bring it on!" The point is that we may think that we can't go in for that one more round, but when we can, it's the greatest feeling ever. This is the purpose of the book, in a nutshell. The point I am trying to make here is that having been equipped with the power of God due to being firmly connected to it, we have nothing to fear anymore. We can take this as a second chance and live our dreams. We can take on the world because we know that God is on our side. We also have filled holes in our spirituality, and we know that now we are more than ready to go out swinging. You feel a renewed sense of spirit and energy. You are more driven and motivated. You are hungry for success. God wants us to get to that point where we can be this mentally strong. It is through building, maintaining, and strengthening that bond that we can do amazing things. We, humans, are blessed with a lot of qualities by our Heavenly Father, so we really need to work to build that connection at all times.

It's all about regaining the courage and picking yourself up. You've faced a rough transition, you've connected with God and have evolved as a person. Then you just need to find that God-given courage within you and take on anything and everything coming your way. I've emphasized in this book that it's very important to first make that connection and strengthen it. Transitions and turning points are part and parcel of life. These are times in your life that represent a major change in your life or that of a loved one. All of these transitions and turning points come from God. He wants to see how we respond to these situations. In many ways, you can call life an endurance test. Just for believing in our Lord and Savior Jesus Christ, we are saved for eternity. Eternal life is a blessing, but we can't take it for granted. I will repeat the famous Uncle Ben saying from the Spider-Man comics and movies, "With great power comes great responsibility." It is this power that allows us to be larger than life but also gives us a great moral and ethical responsibility and one other responsibility. That responsibility is to our Lord and Savior Jesus Christ, who has blessed us with eternal salvation. It is very important to realize how important all these are, especially the one towards Christ. These are things we must realize when harnessing that power and courage that comes from God. The mantra we need to live by is to act responsibly. Use that courage from God for the good of mankind rather than the bad. Be a servant of God and not an enemy. These are important things to remember. This is the last chapter, but this chapter is a very important one. It's summing up everything that we have learned and apply it to the most vital objective that is put in front of all of us. The first thing we need to do is move forward and that too with courage. This is the God-given courage, so when another turning point or transition comes, you are very ready for it and know what to do. You are not thrown off-guard, and you've held tightly to the rope of God. The point of the book is to make you ready for these transitions and turning points. That comes from the evolution that takes place when we are connected with our Lord and Savior, Jesus Christ, and walk His path. When we go down that path, we will feel renewed and refreshed. No matter what issues life throws us, whatever hurdles and problems that come our way, we will be very much prepared. I've mentioned previously in the book that these transitions and turning points in your life are a reminder that everything good and bad comes from God and that He is in control of our lives. We are not in charge of our lives. God has given us life, so he knows our ultimate destiny, and we can only guess. We just have to follow His path, and we will be able to take on everything with complete courage and confidence. Then, just like Rocky, we will go the distance because the ultimate power in the world is by our side! Just like Rocky never gave up, so shall we never give up on holding on to the rope of God.

You should never lose this grip that you have held to the rope of our Lord and Savior, Jesus Christ, no matter what happens. We will be shaken by a lot that happens in our lives, from job losses to loved ones departing to issues with spouses, and so on. Everything here is something we will face because life is finite. Since life is finite, we need to live the way of God. We need to follow the footsteps of our Lord and Savior Jesus Christ. This is the only way to our Heavenly Father, and there is absolutely no other way. That is the way to the Truth and the Light. If that is what you want to pursue, and I urge everyone reading this to make this your life's biggest goal, then you need to hold on to His rope very tightly. You need to keep holding on, no matter what tragedy happens.

Finally, I must tell you is to never have fear. Only fear God, and that is out of respect. When you regain that edge by following the ways of the prophets as described in this book, then you need to be as courageous as them. It's never too late to turn to God, and everyone deserves a second chance. If you are like I was at the time of my job loss, then you absolutely deserve a second chance. If that's the case, then you know what to do.

Thank you for being part of this amazing journey and believe me and more than that, believe God that there will be miracles when you believe. It all starts from the faith; good luck in life, and stay blessed all of you!

I will leave you all with lyrics to an inspirational song from the Disney movie "The Prince of Egypt" as performed by the late great diva Whitney Houston and her contemporary- the living legend and icon Mariah Carey. Hopefully, you will see miracles when you believe!

About the Author

Scot Thomas is a man who wears many hats. He is the Director of Centre for Christian Destiny, Inc., and also a Minister at Hope Christian Fellowship Church. He is also the CEO of Metonymy Consulting, Inc. He holds a Bachelor of Arts degree in English, a Master of Arts degree in Organizational Behavior, and a Ph.D. in Organizational Leadership. Scot's only major achievement and ongoing goal in life is to assist the less fortunate, encourage the broken-hearted, and empower the abandoned. He is unique, creative, and passionate, and it shows in his work. The theme of his work is "Rediscovering your personal edge." It's about getting lost regaining your lost edge. When he was writing his book, he knew that it was time to help people to rediscover their motivation to achieve the impossible by trusting that God could lead them to rediscover the edge that they had lost through life's various challenges.

He wants to let others know that no matter what happened yesterday, there will be a better tomorrow if you want it bad enough, and you can be a better person too if you want to consciously make that change. Scot is a firm believer that we are in this world for a temporary period, so we should spend our time serving God and his people.

Scott Thomas would love to hear thoughts and feedback on his book. He can be reached out at Innercourt@verizon.net, www.centreforchristiandestiny.org His LinkedIn profile is located at https://www.linkedin.com/in/scotrojethomas/

www.ingramcontent.com/pod-product-compliance
Lightning Source LLC
LaVergne TN
LVHW020042110826
845155LV00029B/604
* 9 7 8 1 9 5 0 5 7 6 9 1 3 *